David Keevil was born in 1965 and grew up in the Lancashire town of Oldham, where he still lives. David lives with his wife, Elaine, and their Jack Russell Terrier, Charlie. When he is not working, he enjoys walks through the local countryside with Charlie and his grandsons. His two passions in life are Elvis Presley and *Star wars*. He is a fan of local football and watches Oldham Athletic.

To my wife, Elaine, who gave me the confidence to write this story.

David Keevil

EXCALIBUR'S GOLD

AUSTIN MACAULEY PUBLISHERS™

LONDON • CAMBRIDGE • NEW YORK • SHARJAH

This is a work of fiction. Names, characters, businesses, places, events, locales, and incidents are either the products of the author's imagination or used in a fictitious manner. Any resemblance to actual persons, living or dead, or actual events is purely coincidental.

A CIP catalogue record for this title is available from the British Library.

ISBN 9781398408944 (Paperback)
ISBN 9781398409361 (ePub-e-book)

www.austinmacauley.com

First Published 2022
Austin Macauley Publishers Ltd®
1 Canada Square
Canary Wharf
London
E14 5AA

Prologue

Sometime in the ninth century, a traveller named Owain Llaw Gyffes was wandering around the Welsh countryside looking for work. As he saw daylight appear from the edges of the woods he was leaving, he heard a commotion from down in the valley below. He ran to the edge of the hill to see three rough-looking men attacking a much older weaker looking man. Owain picked up a big fallen branch and ran down the hill screaming at the top of his voice swinging the branch above his head.

He caught the men off their guard, and after Owain had laid out two of his mates, the third fled along the dusty horse path. Owain helped up the old man who surprised him by allowing his muggers to escape scot-free. As the muggers ran off after their mate, the old man picked up his walking stick which was made of Hazelwood and led Owain over to a rock by the side of the path and sat down.

He thanked Owain for saving his life and told him that in his gratitude he would make him a rich man. Owain laughed at him and told him that he didn't save him for any reward; he was just a simple traveller and only needed money to eat. The old man looked up at his saviour and shook his hand. "Indeed you are the man I must tell my secret," the old man told him. Owain looked down at him and asked him what secret?

The old man stood up and leant on his Hazelwood staff and hobbled along the path and pointed to a mountain about a day's walk from them.

"Halfway up that mountain you will find an old oak tree; you can't miss it as it is the only oak tree on the mountain, beneath the oak tree you will find a small hole, just big enough to squeeze through. It may not look big enough for you to get through but don't judge it, try to get through and get through, you will.

"Once under the tree, you will find a small cavern walk about 20 horses length, and you will reach a wall covered in green moss behind the wall you will find a secret passage. Go through the secret passage and you will enter a bigger brighter cavern, but beware the golden bell."

"The golden bell," Owain asked. "What golden bell?"

"The golden bell of Modred," the old man replied. "It hangs above the second doorway; do not touch it, for if you touch it, you will awaken him and his men."

"Who and his men?" Owain asked gingerly.

"Arthur and his men, they sleep beneath the hills waiting until their country needs them again."

Owain looked at the old man's face; surely he wasn't being serious, King Arthur and the Knights of the Round Table. Owain being quite a bright person had heard all the legends about Arthur but surely that's all they were, legends. But something on the old man's face told him that the old man himself believed the story so he kept his silence and listened to what the old man told him.

"They sleep in the cavern, a cavern such as you would never believe existed, for even though it was deep underground the cavern was well lit at all times through the gold and silver on the walls." On the mention of gold and silver, the old man knew that he had Owain's attention now.

"You can fill your purse up with all the gold and silver you wish but don't touch the shield or the sword and do not touch the bell. If you touch the bell and they wake up you must answer No Sleep On, for if you don't answer with those exact words then you would be slain on the spot."

Owain didn't believe in Arthur's legend but he did believe in gold and silver. He asked the old man to accompany him to the mountain but the old man refused his offer telling him that he had been there once and you could only go the once. Owain smiled as the old man hobbled along the path in the opposite direction away from the mountain.

He didn't totally believe the old man's story but towards the mountain was the way he was already going to take so what harm would it be to take a look, besides he had nothing to lose but quite a lot to gain. He smiled and shook his head at the old man's claim of people sleeping under the mountains for close to three centuries. He seemed so sincere in the way that he was telling his story; perhaps the muggers hit him too many times on his head.

It took Owain a good day and a half to reach the mountain and he soon found the oak tree. On finding the hole beneath it, he thought that there was no way on earth that he would squeeze through it. But on hearing the old man's words in his head he knelt down and looked into the hole. He placed his hands in front of his head and shoved them into the hole then followed with his head.

He could feel the cold dirty earth rub along his shoulders as he shoved and shoved to no avail. Then just as he was about to give up he dug his elbows into the sides to give him some leverage and as he pushed, the sides of the hole seemed to move and the hole fitted over him as if he was putting on a jumper. A surprised look came over his face as he slid through the hole and fell into a wide cavern.

He dusted himself down and got up to his feet. He could hardly see a thing so he felt for the wall and made his way down the cavern until he could feel some soft moss on the wall. On feeling the moss, he reached through it and found the secret passage.

On walking through it, he saw the glare of light coming from the end of the passage. At the end of the passage, he noticed a big golden bell hanging over the doorway. He reached out to feel the bell, and as he felt it, it gave out a small clang. "Is it day?" he heard a voice cry out.

Shocked to hear a voice, he looked down to the floor where he saw a man clad in silver armour getting to his feet. Owain quickly remembered what the old man had told him to say, "No, sleep on," he cried. To which the man in armour settled back to his slumber.

Owain couldn't believe his eyes, the legend was true for around the floor of the cavern were 14 knights in armour and one of them had a glistening shield and a sword by his side. His mind was racing for he knew that he was in the presence of something out of this world. Beneath him slept a man of greatness such greatness that he didn't seem worthy of him to be in the same room. He quietly looked around the cavern the floor in the middle was covered in mounds of gold and silver oddments with all the knights sleeping around them.

And the walls, the walls were of such beauty, beauty the like of which he had never seen, nor was likely to see again. The walls were what made the room bright, for they seemed to be made of silver and gold. He filled up his purse with a handful of golden coins that lay on the floor. Then he placed a massive silver and pearl necklace around his neck and walked around waving his hands in the air cheering.

He remembered what the old man told him about not being too greedy and only being allowed in the once. Owain wasn't a greedy man but on seeing all the riches around him it went to his head. He took off his shirt and filled it with whatever it would hold and once it was almost too heavy to pull the set off out of the cavern.

But his mind was racing with what he was going to do with all this treasure that he forgot about the bell and headbutted it on his way out. The clang was so loud that all the knights awoke and staggered to their feet, "Is it day?" they asked in unison.

Owain couldn't speak as he saw the lumbering body of King Arthur get to his feet with a sword in hand. On hearing no answer, all the knights waded into poor Owain and ripped him limb from limb. As the last cry left Owain's body, the knights settled back into their slumber. The last thing he saw before he died was green moss tightening up in front of the passage and the light from the walls slowly dimmed to darkness.

Chapter One
The Journal

2008. The present-day, a newly married couple Alex and Julie Ferns were on the way to Barrow-in-Furnace in the Lake District to buy a painting that her great-great-great-great-grandfather Frederick Concerve had painted in 1849. It was a painting of the Britannia Bridge across the Menai Strait in North Wales. They had found an old journal that Concerve had written telling them about a great treasure being hidden and the first clue was shown on the painting.

"Are you sure about this?" Alex asked. "There must be something strange about this, I mean at auction he could get almost a million pounds for this painting and he's letting it go for a measly 20 grand."

"Some people don't realise the value of things hidden before their eyes, after all, who'd have thought that we would get 13 million pounds for our painting of The Rainhill Trials."

"After what we went through for that, we deserved every penny; it's just that he sounded strange over the phone."

"He wasn't strange; he was Scottish; and I told you, he just wants a quick sale because he had to leave the country in a hurry, why he had to leave isn't our concern, our only concern is to retrieve my families painting, here we are it should be just around the corner."

They parked up the car and walked towards the cottage where a small gentleman was waiting for them. As Julie spoke to the man who introduced himself as Ian, Alex walked over to the two cars that were parked in the drive. One was an old 1970s Hillman Imp, and the other was a red Jaguar XJR and it caught Alex's eye straight away.

"You can have that an all," Ian shouted over to him. "Another 20 grand and it's yours."

"I can't believe that you did that," Julie told him. "We only came for the picture and now we are going home with a big red car, I mean can you actually drive that thing, especially with your history."

"I'm a safe driver, remember it was Pete who caused that accident, besides let's call it your wedding present to me."

"And what's my present from you?"

Alex smiled and replied, "The painting of course."

On completing the deal for the car and the painting, they bid goodbye to Ian and drove into the village to book into a guest house for the night. After having their supper, they settled down in their room. "While you watch the telly, I'll have another read of Concerve's journal to see if we have missed anything out before we set off for Wales in the morning. As Julie sat back to watch TV, Alex laid back on the bed and opened up Concerve's tatty journal.

To whoever is reading this hopefully, you are one of my descendants as only a descendant of mine would be able to find the first clue. First, let me introduce myself I am Frederick Concerve. I was a surveyor and designer working for my good friend Robert Stephenson and his father George. But long since retired, my wife Juliet and I retired to Yorkshire to live in house that I myself designed. The first few years were splendid living in our house in the middle of the moors. No one could have asked for a more bliss existence.

I was born into a family with barely a sixpence to bless ourselves with and look me now living in a big cottage that I built on land I own. I was happy in my cottage, away from all the interlopers and usurpers of the big towns who looked down at me because they were born to money.

And just cause they had money they thought them better than me. I moved into the cottage because my wife had come ill I thought that air around here would soothe her but the winters here were very brisk and too cold for a woman as weak as Juliet. She died in the first spring following another winter cut off from all mankind. And she was closely followed by my young son George who died of fever at age of 13.

All I now had was my daughter Lizzy but she had been betrothed to a local farmer, a gentle but strong man named Patrick Ashcroft. I knew she be well cared for so when I received a visit in the spring of 52 from my friend Robert I jumped at chance to help him on his latest project.

He had been summoned by the NWNGR and the Festiniog Railway Company to build a railway to Porthmadog from the slate mines and copper mines deep in the Welsh mountains. He was working with Charles Easton Spooner who was the chief engineer of the Festiniog railway and Croesor Tramway.

I came out of retirement, not for money; I had enough of that to last me out. I helped him, because he was my friend. Nay friend, more like a brother for we were both born and bred in same North East village and we grew up together. He liked to have a fellow Geordie with him and at least I could understand his father. The money people disliked the Stephenson's because they were self-made and they didn't need their money to solve any problems that may happen. If a problem arose and no cure be then start afresh and build a solution, that was their motto and it served them fine.

Anyway our last job together is where we struck lucky more than we knew. There were five of us altogether journeying that fateful day. Myself, Robert, a money man Elias Farthingay and two surveyors from the NWNGR, Patrick Bracegirdle and John Brones.

I had dealings with Farthingay before. He was a money man and I took him as untrustworthy. He wanted the line made as quick and cheap as could be. But Robert didn't work like that, to him safety come first especially after having one of his bridges collapse and cause folk death. But Farthingay wasn't like us the blessedness of giving was yet unknown to him because he gave unwillingly.

But Bracegirdle and Brones I didn't know. Truly the NWNGR had sent us two of the most unusual looking men around. John Brones was a man of about 45, rather below the medium height, stout and florid, his face was not by any means prepossessing, it narrowed upwards as through the lord had been trying out a new shape and not with the most satisfying result.

For his heavy jaw and square chin seemed out of proportion with his narrow retreating forehead, his eyes were small and too close together, all in all, he wasn't the most attractive of men. Patrick wasn't much better he was a rickety man, tall and thin, too thin for his bones were sticking out. He looked like he needed a good meal in him, but he did eat, by the lord did he eat. He could eat a full cob without soup. He was thin for another reason and we all knew that he didn't have much longer with us. Looking at them both for the first time you would think the freak show was in town.

After taking the locomotive to Porthmadog, we had a day's travel by horse and cart to reach the copper mines just past the Aberglaslyn Pass. It was rich with copper but the only way back to the seaport of Madog was by horse and it was too long and slow a journey to money make so the only option was a railway. We set up camp at the base of one of the surrounding mountains and settled down for the night. Even though it was the beginning of summer it was cold sleeping in the mountains.

The next morning, we went off to do a survey on the mountain pass to see if it was build-worthy. No matter which way we tried it would mean cutting a tunnel through one of the mountains maybe two. So we made our way up the closest one to check the earth. As we walked up, it we came across an old dead oak tree, must have been there for centuries, all that now stood was an old decaying stump. Bracegirdle had the bright idea to try to remove the stump and then we would get a better idea of the density of the earth. So we pulled and pushed at it and as it was giving Bracegirdle gave out a cry as the ground gave way and he slipped into a cavern under the stump.

We hurriedly rushed to his aid but we couldn't see him. We cried out to him and we were much relieved when we heard him cry back. We lit the lamps and carefully dropped downhole, where we found Bracegirdle nursing a badly broken shin. His bones were so weak with an illness that he was lucky not to have snapped his back. Once we had carried him to the surface, we went back down to inspect the cavern. It stretched for about a hundred yards then we came to a dead end. We were about to go back to the daylight when Robert leant against the mossy wall and fell through it.

"Come ye quick," we heard him shout. "There's another way out, I see daylight."

Brones was the first to follow, then Farthingay then me, I was a tad wary about going any deeper as to me if the lord had wanted us to live underground he would have gave us eyes like owls so we could see. We followed the light but it didn't lead to the outside, the light itself wasn't daylight but a bright glare that shone from walls.

There was a big metal bell hung on the top of the passageway to the big bright cavern, and once in it, we couldn't believe our eyes. There were the bodies of 14 men all dressed in armour, well bodies wasn't correct for all that was in the armour was dust.

"Must be a burial mould," Brones cried as we spotted two piles of gold and silver oddments in the centre of the cavern.

Robert was more interested in the walls where the glare from it was lighting up the cavern. "I think it's gold," he told us as he took a scraping from it. "It's not copper, nor silver."

"Truly sins harvest had ripened quickly," Farthingay cried as he picked up a gold mask that was with the oddments on the floor while Brones inspected the shield and sword of one of the knights.

"Why waste time on him, he's dustman," Farthingay shouted to him. "Help me pack some of this in here." Brones ignored him and held his lamp closer to the shield. "Oh my lord," he cried. "It's Arthur, King Arthur."

"Don't be a foolish man," Farthingay cried. "That's just an old myth and legend."

"It's Arthur, I tell you," Brones cried as I and Robert knelt down by his side. "Look at his shield, his sword it's got Arthur's shibboleth on it, the black crow and the image of the virgin. The virgin as the badge of the ideal Christian leader against the pagan foe and Arthur was told that when he died he would return as a big black bird, it's Arthur I tell you."

Now Brones was an educated man we were told and he knew his history, but Arthur, Camelot and the Knights of the Round Table, it couldn't be. I didn't believe it but for some reason Robert did. "We have to leave this place, you have to believe me," Brones warned us.

"B'lieve, b'lieve I do not b'lieve in myths, legends," Farthingay replied. "Only thing that's true is money; money speaks in this day and age."

"It's cursed its sacred land," Brones shouted to him but Farthingay just smiled at him and told him that it wasn't sacred land; it was the land of the NWNGR. "It'll cover the cost of the railway and more," he sneered. "If it was gold on the walls then it must be a gold mine, a gold mine on our land can you believe it."

"You can't build on here, it's cursed and it'll be the end of us all. Build a tunnel through here and mark my words it'll collapse, it'll kill people."

"There's always a chance of that, no matter where we build, ask yon laddie there."

"That bridge was an accident," Robert cried at him. "The steel wasn't right, I didn't know."

"I'm not blaming you," Farthingay replied. "I'm just saying that accidents happen no matter how careful people be, but there's no way that we are leaving all this here, it'll be worth a fortune."

"But it's not ours," Robert told him. "This lot belongs to the Welsh, it's their heritage."

"The Welsh be hanged," Farthingay replied.

"But it's not your say, that be four of us down here," Brones told him.

"Impudent puppy," Farthingay shouted to Brones. "I own you, you do as I say."

"You do not own me; I work for you that is all."

"Work for me, you do as I say or work for me no more, p'haps educated you be but as long as you work for me you do as I say."

Robert and I sided with Brones, but Farthingay wasn't for yielding. He told us that if nature had endowed us with such a gift then he thought it ought to be cultivated then he turned on his heels and marched away and ascended up the passageway to breathe some much-needed fresh air. As he left the cavern, we carried out a further survey of what was in the cave and on the back wall I found a small lead cross. It was about a foot high and the writing was in Latin.

As it be, Brones was a scholar in the language. He could barely contain his delight as he informed us of what it told.

King Arthur's
Burial Cross

HIC IACET SEPULTUS INCLYTUS REX ARTURIES.
In English, it reads
HERE THE GREAT KING ARTHUR LIES BURIED

"It could be a fake," Robert told him.

"Who would fake a burial cross and then hide it, it does not make sense," Brones replied. "I tell you it's Arthur and we must leave him be."

"There's written word on the bell too," Robert told us as he shone his lamp up to the glistening bell hung above the passageway.

Brones got to his feet and looked up to the bell. "What does it say?" I asked them both.

"It's another warning," Brones replied. IF THOU HAD DRAWN THE SWORD OR RAISED SHIELD THOU HAD BEEN UNLUCKIEST MAN EVER BORN.

"We must leave it all here, promise me you will not let Farthingay take any of it, he is not historian he will empty this place to fill his own coffers, it is not up to us, it is the responsibility of the Welsh, not us English, please help me to preserve it. It's been there for centuries who are we to say what must be taken, it's a place of worship not gain."

Robert held up the sword to my lamp as he inspected it. It was glided all along with silver and gold. "So you tell me that this is Excalibur," he asked of Brones. "It does not look centuries old, it looks like it is made yesterday."

"Place it back be with the shield," Brones cried. "It is not meant to be handled by the common man, it is a sword for kings, it's, well, it's Arthur's child and we cannot part it from him."

"Are you still sprouting that gibberish?" Farthingay cried as he reappeared through the passageway. "I've told you what we do, we take everything we can carry if you say it's for a king to behold then all this gilt will make me king."

Brones looked disgusted with the haughty airs of Farthingay and warned him once again about removing anything from sacred ground.

Farthingay just looked at him and smiled as he reached up to unhook the gold bell. "This'll cover the cost of at least two locomotives," he cried as the bell clanged on the touch of the ground as it was heavier than he had imagined. "Put it back," Brones shouted as he grabbed hold of Farthingay's shoulder.

"Unhand me, you erth," Farthingay shouted as he pulled out his whip.

"You dare lay hands on a gentleman," he cried as he whipped Brones across the face. In the act of defending himself, he charged into Farthingay and pushed him face first against the glistening glare of the wall.

As they fell to the floor, Robert and I reached between them and pulled them apart. "You scoundrel," Farthingay shouted.

"I'll see you flogged, I'll…" Farthingay stopped in mid-sentence and threw his hands up to his face. "I can't see, I can't see," he screamed. "What have you done? I can't see."

Robert told him to shut up and keep still while he checked him over. "Probably just gold dust in your eye, it'll clear, come on I'll lead you to daylight."

"It wasn't me," Brones shouted. "I never touched him, I was defending myself."

I tried to reassure him that Farthingay would be alright but he kept blabbering on about us being in a cursed place, "We should not have removed the bell, he has doomed us all."

As I left the cavern to seek daylight, I looked back to see Brones struggling to lift the bell back up, I thought about helping him but before I could do out there be a loud roar from the roof of the cavern and the whole place began to cave in. I looked helplessly as Brones' head got flattened by falling rock. He was gonna and so was I if I did not quickly get out. With a helping hand from my good friend Robert, I managed to escape the cave in.

We stood there Robert and me in silence as we realised that we did not have the tools for the mighty dig that it would take to free Brones from the rock. We decided to leave him there. He did not have no family to speak of, he would not be missed, besides we thought that to be buried with a king he would have wanted.

There was nothing we could do for Farthingay's sight; he was blinded by the dust from the wall. He kept us up all night with his childish howling, if either of us wouldn't have been us then maybe we would have put him out of his misery there and then. We thought about it but we were no killers Robert and I, we thought that all men deserved a chance to live even blind greedy men like Farthingay. All we wanted was to get away from this place, me to my cottage him to his factory. We needed to keep Bracegirdle warm or he would not make the dawn either. There was no way that we could travel through the mountain pass in the dark so we had to wait for the first light.

We got what lamps we had and poured the oil from them over the Oak stump and set it ablaze. We rested poor Bracegirdle's broken body next to the heat and waited for the day. While Bracegirdle and Farthingay slept, I and Robert decided that no one must know about our find, especially not the greedy men of the NWNGR. We couldn't trust Farthingay to keep his quiet so in the morning we tied a rope around the stump and dragged its roots and all along the pass until it was well clear of the mountain that it had lain on for centuries.

But I jest you not when we left the campsite after the cave in I looked back and I saw a big black crow sitting on the top of the mound of earth that now hid the entrance to the cave. It was staring straight at me, I did not believe the legend that Arthur on death turned into a big black bird but on seeing the crow there at that time it damn near sent a shiver running down my spine, and that's when it hit me that we did the right thing in leaving the treasure behind. It was too much for any one man and Robert and I did not want it. There will come a time in the future when the people of Wales will need a lift and nothing would be more powerful than the sword Excalibur to lift the spirit of a nation.

As we rode the cart back to Porthmadog, poor Bracegirdle sadly passed away. He was too feeble and broken to recover but at least unlike Brones he would be transported back to his loved ones for a final goodbye. We did not believe in curses Robert and me but five of us set off that morning and on finding the hidden treasure only two of us would have any life after it. As we arrived in the seaport tired and downhearted, the mighty sea birds were trilling forth their jubilant songs as though there were no such thing as sickness or death. But we knew better.

The railway was eventually finished, Robert stayed behind to make sure that King Arthur's treasure would never be discovered, well not by the greedy anyway.

Robert didn't want anything to do with the treasure. He was superstitious and thought it best to stay hidden. He had worked all his life to get where he was and he thought his kin would feel the same. So it was his idea to leave it and somehow work the railroad around so as not to disturb the cavern.

Farthingay though blinded lived on and delighted in his free ale as he told of his mighty find in the valleys hidden. He told all he knew to his brother Jeremiah who took it upon himself to find the treasure. Jeremiah was his brother's brother; he liked his drink, his women and most of all his money. The only problem was he did not know how to keep it.

Eventually, after Farthingay's death, Jeremiah came calling first to Robert and then to me, pleading with us to lead him back to the cavern. We told him that there was no treasure and that it was part of the madness of his brother's blindness. He never did believe us and I heard that he spent the rest of his life in the Welsh mountains desperately trying to find the cavern, without success. He eventually got knifed in the back and his body was found in the waters of Beddgelert. But not before documenting everything he knew and everywhere he had searched in his journals.

Robert and I decided that only the worthy would be able to go for Arthur's cavern so we have left seven clues to the whereabouts of the mountain. I left the first clue in my painting of the Britannia Bridge on Anglesey. The first clue will take you to Roberts first clue which leads to my second clue and so on. I suppose you wonder why I don't just tell you the location but life's not so simple, you don't get out for free and I ought to know. I have worked for everything I have and worked bloody hard so if you want to be rich then you also will have to work and I'm going to make you work hard.

There are certain rules to be learnt about your quest. On finding cavern, I only ask that you leave the bell where it lay, for definitely cursed it be for the two of us to touch it bad thing happened to. The shield and the sword are the property of the Welsh people and must be returned to them so as the people of Wales can be given hope and pride in their country. The gold and silver oddments can be shared between whoever finds it but be warned of the greedy man and the Light Being Man for he was the most dangerous of obstacles to overcome. Now here is where I leave you but follow my directions, find my painting of the building of the Britannia Bridge and a great treasure you will find.

Chapter Two
Britannia Bridge

Building the
Britannia Bridge

After finishing the journal, Alex asked Julie if she thought that Arthur actually existed.

"There is a legend," Julie told him. "That stated that after losing his faith after winning the battle against his son Mordred, Arthur and his men took to a secret cave where they sleep until their country needed them again.

"Obviously, that's a crock of shit, because where were they in the Neapolitan war, the Crimean War and the two World Wars, nowhere. But that doesn't mean he never existed because history confirms that he did and he did own a sword called Excalibur.

"The sword was magnificent, not gold nor silver but gilded with very fine decorations and made with the finest materials known at the time. Now Concerve has written that he had found a cave that had a golden bell hanging over the doorway and that there were 14 suits of armour on the floor, one with a decorated sword and shield.

"Now that was over a hundred years ago but the armour, sword and shield were still intact even though they had been buried for over ten centuries.

"So if they were indeed intact after so long then another 150 years wouldn't have corroded them much. The only problem was that there were many mountains in Wales most of which have old railways on them and some with tunnels through them.

"But Concerve was only surveying the hills so we can't even be sure that the cavern was near a railway line especially after what he says about preserving the treasure for mankind. So to answer your question I don't believe in Arthur the legend but I do believe in my great, great, great, great grandfather Frederick Concerve and if there's a treasure in far hills then we will go for it."

"But Excalibur was handed to the Lady in the Lake on Arthur's death," Alex told her. "So how could it go with him to his grave?"

"The Lady in the Lake is just part of folklore, she didn't really exist."

"And Merlin, did he exist?"

"Yes, Merlin did exist but he wasn't a wizard with great power he was most probably a soothsayer or prophet, or just a very clever man who was too intelligent for that age."

"So what are we looking for exactly?"

"If it does exist we will do as Concerve wanted, we will hand the sword and shield to the Welsh people, leave the bell where it was and share the rest between all the charities we can find in Wales."

"So we don't get a penny?"

"As Concerve stated, he didn't need the money and at this moment in time thanks to your grandfather we are sorted for life and all. The man riches he craves life he didn't live."

"Meaning?"

"If money is all that you want then the money is all that you get, you don't have time to live, to love, all your time was taken making more money. Remember Concerve's words. Beware the greedy man for he is the most dangerous of foes."

"I'm not a greedy man but there's gonna be expenses."

"We have still over 12 million pounds from the painting, think of it, we are not doing this for the money, it's the chase we are after, we are Historians, you have spent your life in that art gallery swooning over pieces of art that you could never even touch. We have got the chance to find the greatest artefact of all time Excalibur. Our names will be embraced in history."

Alex looked at her and smiled, "Just as long as I don't get shot this time."

"There's no one to shoot you, there is no one else after it remembers everyone was dead who was connected to conserve's story."

"Just as long as it wasn't just a story, where do we start?"

"We first have to find the clue that he hid in this painting and then we head to deepest Anglesey for our belated honeymoon, my love."

They had a good look at the painting but nothing stood out. "We will have to compare the painting with the real-life bridge to see if anything pops out," Julie told him.

A week later after sorting everything out back in the Yorkshire village of Rishworth where they now lived they headed off to the Isle of Anglesey where they had rented a cottage near the village of Mona. After settling into the cottage, they had a quiet night in the local Inn before retiring for the night and starting their trek in the morning.

In the morning, they had a drive to the bridge but then realised that they needed to look at it from the same angle as the painting so they drove along the A55 until the bridge looked the same size as the painting. They then left the car in the lay-by and walked down the green fields until it matched up to the spot where Concerve painted his picture.

A shiver ran through Julie's body as she realised that she stood on the very spot where her Great ancestor stood over 150 years before. For some reason, tears came to her eyes and she started to cry. Alex hugged her as he understood her reasons for crying as he felt the exact same when he stood on the grounds of the old POW camp where his great grandfather was held in World War II.

"Something's not right," he told her as the bridges somehow didn't match. "It's a different bridge."

"It can't be?" Julie cried as she desperately looked at the painting then the bridge. "Shit," she cried as she realised that indeed it was a different bridge.

"Old one must have been destroyed years ago," Alex told her. "Probably a fire or a bomb in the war."

"Either way it's not there now," she replied. "It's over; I can't believe it's over before we even started."

"Nothing over yet," Alex told her. "Remember our quest for the Rainhill Trials, we thought it was finished because the cottage wasn't where it should have been, but we persevered, and eventually, we found it."

"But the cottage was still standing; the bridge isn't so how can we carry on from here?" Alex threw an arm around her and pointed to the mountains over the estuary in Wales and told her that if Excalibur was hidden in one of those mountains then we will find it, he didn't know how, but they would find it. He wiped her tears away, put the painting back in its leather case and then walked back up the field to the lay-by.

"Holy crap," Alex shouted as they discovered that their newly bought red Jaguar XJR had been stolen. "Can this day get any worse?" Julie cried as Alex went running down the A55 trying to spot his car.

They couldn't even phone the police because Alex's mobile phone was left in the cottage charging up and Julie's battery was too low. They eventually managed to flag a lift back to their cottage in Mona. Seeing as they had no transport they decided to relax and spend a couple of days together away from their quest. After all, it was their honeymoon.

Within the week, their car got recovered and they drove to the port town of Holyhead to do some research in the local library, where they discovered that the Britannia Bridge was destroyed by fire in 1970 and rebuilt. It reopened to rail traffic in 1972 and road later in 1980. Distraught they headed back to the cottage to ponder their next move.

As Julie poured him a stiff drink, Alex looked at a map of North Wales. "Just think," he told her. "Underneath one of these mountains lies what we seek."

Julie handed him his drink as he pointed down on the map. "We know what area it's in," he told her. "It's between Porthmadog and either Beddgelert or Ffestiniog, we could just ignore the clues and search the mountains."

"Like Farthingay did," Julie replied. "For years without finding out."

"Yeah, but we have better equipment."

"Equipment won't help us, besides if we do this we are gonna do it properly, the way Concerve shows us."

"Your call, you're the boss."

"It'll be easier Concerve's way," she told him as she pointed to the map. "Because in the circular 30 miles from Porthmadog there were over 40 hills and mountains. It'll take us years if we're lucky to find the right one. To comb each one further would take weeks, maybe months at a time on each one, especially with 150 years of natural growth over the cavern. Even with Concerve's instructions, we would be lucky to strike gold."

They then checked out all the existing railway lines around the mountains. They found existing lines from Porthmadog to Dolgellau, Barmouth, Caernarfon, Pwllheli, and Ffestiniog.

"Dolgellau, Ffestiniog and Caernarfon pass through those mountains," Julie told him. "So we can rule out the mountains that those railways pass through as Stephenson wouldn't have built so close to the site in case it was unearthed in the excavation."

"Good, then that only leaves us with about 37 to search," Alex replied with a sly grin on his face.

As they spent the evening having a quiet drink in the garden, Alex suddenly had a thought and jumped up. "What's up?" Julie shouted as she followed him into the cottage.

"Remember The Rainhill Trials, my great-grandfather hid the painting in the back of another painting, I know it's too much of a coincidence but what if the clue's not in the painting itself but inside the painting, on the back of it." They retrieved the painting from the back and gently placed it front down on the table.

"Here goes," Alex told her as he carefully pulled the back off the frame.

"Nothing," Julie cried as the back of the painting was bare. "It was a good thought but."

"Look," Alex cried as he interrupted her. On the inside of the back of the frame was some writing, very old writing and Alex recognised the hand of Concerve as the writer.

"What does it say?" Julie asked as Alex pulled a lamp towards it.

"In 1849, a bridge was built to carry the locomotives over the valley in West Ridings Yorkshire, over the river near a village of cotton. In archway where the river flows, halfway up there be straight and narrow on top of etchings lay that you need to see."

"West Ridings of Yorkshire," Julie cried. "We going back home, the bugger has left a clue near home."

"Bloody hell," cried Alex. "That's so obvious, there wasn't much transport in that day so the clues must all be quite close to where he and Stephenson either lived or worked."

"What's a straight and narrow anyway?" Julie asked him.

"Presumably something that's narrow but extremely straight," Alex replied with a smile on his face.

"Very funny," she cried as she playfully punched his shoulder.

"Well, I don't know, do I. Could be a ledge but I'll only be guessing, it'll help if your flaming ancestor spoke proper English. The man that only thinks is proper is what he himself speaks is a man who isn't proper to the common man that speaks," Alex smiled at the love of his life as he waited with bated breath for her to explain her little rhyme. She smiled back at him as she told him, "You love me even though I speak gibberish so you are contradicting yourself as you speak." Alex shook his head at her and told her that indeed she was Concerve's kin.

"First thing in the morning we have to set off," Julie told him. "We need a computer to get on the internet; the closest one is back in the flat."

The next day they were back in the flat above Julie's cake shop in Rishworth. "Got it," Alex cried as he pointed at the computer screen. "Only Railway Bridge to be built in West Yorkshire in 1849 was the viaduct over the River Tame just before the entrance to the village of Uppermill."

"I know that place," Julie replied. "That viaduct stands out for miles, it's massive. We can be there in less than half an hour." They grabbed their coats and a camera and drove the 10 miles or so over the Saddleworth Moors to the quiet village of Uppermill.

"I know this place," Alex told her as they drove through the Moors. "This is where Allen tried to run us off the road in our quest for the Rainhill Trials, but it isn't Yorkshire, I thought this was Oldham in Lancashire?"

"That's a long-standing argument some people around here claim to live in Yorkshire others claim Lancashire, Oldham is on the very verge of both as Yorkshire and Lancashire run side by side up the country."

The village of Uppermill is on the northern side of greater Manchester tucked away in a valley in the Pennines four miles to the east of Oldham. The history of the village was dominated by the expansion of wool and cotton spinning into the area during the Industrial Revolution with several mills being constructed. The mills that fed the population have long since disappeared, either being knocked down or converted into luxury flats to accommodate a new generation of high-class workers who wouldn't know what hard labour was unlike the former tenants of the village.

Alex could see the viaduct way before they reached it but as they couldn't park up anywhere near it they carried on into the small village of Uppermill. They finally found a parking place in a car park next to a small museum on the side of the canal. They decided to walk along the canal path rather than back up the high street. After walking for about 10 minutes, they reached a small bridge that crossed over the canal just before a lock that carried on just after the viaduct. They walked underneath the viaduct where the canal flowed and looked up into the arches. "Right," said Alex. "What exactly are we looking for?"

"A straight and narrow that lies halfway up," Julie replied.

"Must mean that ledge," Alex told her as he pointed to a ledge that was just above a row of seven large blocks that ran along the underside of the arch. Alex zoomed his camera into the ledge but there was no way at all to see what if anything was written along the top.

"What are those seven blocks sticking out under the ledge?" Julie asked.

"Some sort of support girders I guess," Alex replied. "They must run quite a distance inside the brickwork to support the size of this Viaduct this big."

"Which ledge would he mean?" Alex asked as he noticed that a ledge was on either side of the arch, one 30 feet above the towpath the other above the canal waters. "The side on the path hopefully," Julie replied. "Because God knows how we'd reach the canal side." In fact, she told him, "How on earth are we going to get up to that ledge off the towpath?"

"There's a metal drain pipe running down this side," Alex cried as he looked from the other side of the bridge. "I think I should be able to shinny up the pipe and reach the ledge and get on to it by swinging my leg over the first block sticking out and pulling myself up."

"Are you sure?" Julie asked as she looked how high it seemed. "Are you any good at climbing?"

"Not as good as Pete was, but I used to climb trees as a kid."

"This isn't a tree, it's high and there's not much room to manoeuvre, plus if you fall there's nowt soft to break your fall."

"I can do this, I can do this, and if you look at the wall there are loads of deep crevasses I can get finger holds in."

He grabbed a hold of the drain pipe and started to climb until Julie told him that some people were walking towards them with a dog on a lead. He jumped down and waited for them to pass. But as they passed another group of ramblers walked towards them, and then another. They decided to wait until dark so they walked back towards the village and found somewhere to get a bite to eat. They saw a sign outside a public house saying food served all day. Julie went inside to order while Alex went to a shop across the road to try to buy a torch.

After their meal, they had a look inside the local museum to see if there was anything about the viaduct. It had a big feature about it but it didn't tell them anything new. After the museum, Alex treated them both to a ride along the canal on a longboat. They cuddled up on the back row of seats in the converted barge and just smiled at each other and enjoyed the tranquil surroundings of the countryside as they slowly drifted by. As they entered the lock underneath the viaduct, Alex leapt up and took some photos of the archway. "I wonder where this clue will lead us?" he whispered to Julie as he gave her a quick peck on her forehead. She smiled at him and held his hand in hers as they looked back at the viaduct.

After they had returned from their journey, they waited for dark to draw in before making their way back up the canal to the viaduct. They sat down at a bench and table a bit further up from the viaduct until they were sure that the coast was clear. "Are you sure about this?" Julie asked. "It's awfully high."

He told her that he'd be fine and started to climb the metal drainpipe. But after about 20 feet, he mumbled something and slid back down. "What's up?" she asked him.

"I forgot to buy a pen and paper," he replied. "What am I gonna write it down on?"

"Hang on," she told him as she searched through her handbag before handing him a pen and a notebook. "Good job one of us came prepared."

He gave her a quick peck on her lips before returning to the drainpipe. "Be careful," she whispered as she watched him shinny up.

He soon reached the level of the drainpipe that was the same height as the ledge, so he rested a while to get his bearings. It seemed a lot higher from up there than what it did from the towpath. "It's further than I thought," he shouted down to her. "I thought that I'd be able to reach the ledge but I can't."

She told him to come down if he thought that it was too dangerous to carry on. He smiled at her and told her he'd be fine.

He leant forward to try to reach the ledge but it was just out of his reach. He could feel his fingernails scrape the edge of it. "I've got an idea," he whispered. "If I go a bit higher, there are some gaps in the archway that I may be able to use as finger holes."

She watched while sucking on her thumb like a nervous kid as her new husband eased his way up the drain pipe.

He wrapped his left arm around the pipe and reached out with his right foot until it found a grip on the beginning of the ledge. He let his arm slip away from the pipe and grasped a firm hold with his hand and edged his foot bit by bit along the ledge until he could go no further, at least not without letting go of the pipe with his hand.

Once he knew that he had a firm footing, he reached up with his right hand and found a gap to get a firm grip. "Shit," Julie cried. "There's somebody coming, turn your torch off."

"Bloody hell," he whispered as he fumbled to turn off the torch. He held firm as Julie slipped into the bushes by the side of the viaduct, waiting anxiously for the young couple to pass.

She shook her head in dismay as the couple sat down on the wall of the small bridge that led over the canal just before the viaduct. She was getting desperate for she knew that Alex couldn't hold on for much longer. Then she sighed with relief as they got up and walked over the bridge and away down the path and out of sight.

Alex had already seen them go and had turned his torch back on but he had gotten a cramp in the hand that he was gripping with so he had no option but to return fully to the drain pipe. He wrapped his arm around it again so that he was secure enough to rub some life back into his fingers. "Are you alright?" she whispered up to him.

"Yeah, just got a touch of cramp, I'll be okay in a sec," he told her. He rubbed his hands together while blowing on them, "Right, I'll try again, wish me luck."

He quickly got back into his original position and this time he managed to grip with both hands. "Shit," she heard him cry. "What's up?" she asked.

"I'm facing the wrong way and the way that the arch was made I haven't got room to stand."

"What can you do?"

"I'll have to try to sit on the ledge and support myself by using the stone girders as footrests and try to work my way across, hopefully, the etching, if there's any, wasn't too far across." Again she sucked on her thumb as she watched him slowly slide his body down the wall of the viaduct and carefully reach out for one of the girders with his right leg.

Once he found the girder, he managed to turn his body around. At least now, he was facing the right way and this way felt a tad more comfortable. He rested awhile and shone his torch along the top of the ledge. "Can you see out?" she shouted.

He whispered down to her to be quiet and then lifted his head up to inspect the ledge. "Nothing yet," he whispered as he slowly reached with his right foot to the next girder. Once he felt it, he manoeuvred his body along the ledge and then moved to the next girder and then the next until suddenly he stopped and started rubbing his fingers over the top of the ledge.

"What is it?" she asked. "Have you found something?"

"There's something," he replied but it's hard to make out. "It's caked in years and years of some kind of mould, I'm trying to scrape it off to make sense of it."

"Be careful, don't forget where you are."

"I'm not stupid."

"You don't have to be stupid to break your neck."

"Well, if I fall, bloody catch me," he replied as he returned to scraping the mould away.

"Bloody hell," she heard him cry.

"What is it?" she asked. "What have you found?"

"It's some sort of emblem," he told her. "There's a shield with a bridge with what looked like an old steam engine and I'm sure it's supposed to be The Rocket."

"The Rocket, Stephenson's Rocket, are you sure?"

"Yeah, definite I can't mistake The Rocket after what we went through." He followed his finger down from the bottom of the emblem and rubbed along the top of the ledge. "There's an etching on top here, but I can't make it out," he told her as he scraped away the moss from it. "It's definitely some writing; it looks like it's in Welsh." He scraped some more to make sure that he had found the full clue, and then he put a piece of paper over pressed down on it and traced over the paper with his pen to make an imprint of the clue. When he thought that he had traced the full message he made a tracing of the emblem. "Right," he shouted. "I think I've got all I need, only thing is, how the hell do I get back down. He told her to catch the torch as he dropped it down to her and shine it along the ledge so he could follow the light back to the pipe.

31

As she shone it up to him, he placed the tracings into his pocket and carefully edged back along the ledge towards safety. "Careful," she shouted as he reached for the pipe with his left hand.

"I can't reach it," he cried. "I'll have to try to turn around and stand up and retrace my original movements."

Alex was worried, more than worried he was God damn frightened he wasn't a man for heights, he was okay going up because he was looking up but now he had to get down he looked down. As he saw the drop below him, he froze. "I can't move," he cried. "I don't know why but I can't move."

Julie held her head in her hands as she tried desperately to think of a way to get her beloved husband down to safety.

"Don't look down," she cried. "Look straight ahead, find something to grip hold of and slowly turn to your side."

"I can't do it, I'm gonna fall, I know I'm gonna fall."

"You're not gonna fall," she shouted.

"I CAN'T MOVE, my arms feel like lead, I haven't the strength to lift them up."

"Alex, calm down, you are not going to fall, calm yourself take a minute. Compose yourself and concentrate all your mind on turning to your right and reaching for a grip."

"I can't, I'll fall."

"You are not going to fall, believe me, you'll be safe, I've got confidence in you, you can do this."

"Are you sure?"

"Course I'm sure, for Christ sake, you have survived a head-on car crash with a massive truck and being shot and knifed by a maniac, if God had wanted you dead, you'd be dead now, so stop messing about, turn around, stand up and grab hold of that bloody drain pipe, I'm dying of thirst down here and the pubs will be shutting soon."

A smile came to his face, "I do love you," he told her.

"I love you too," she replied. "More than life itself, so grab that pipe, come down here and love me some more."

"Right," he cried as he composed himself and took a deep breath. Julie stuck her thumb back into her mouth as she watched him slowly turn to his right.

"That's it," she told him. "Now try to stand up." He slowly pulled himself up. "Now get a grip."

He got a good grip with both hands and slowly made his way along the ledge towards the drain pipe.

"You're doing well," she shouted. "Now try to reach with your left hand for the pipe."

He managed to grab the pipe and Julie sighed with relief as he wrapped his arm around it. "Right you're almost there now," she told him. "Now slide your foot over and you're home and dry."

Once he had safely reached the drain pipe, it was just a case of him sliding down it to the towpath.

"I'm sorry about that," he whispered as she hugged him at the bottom. "I felt strange, scared even."

"You're alright now," she cried. "You're safe now."

He showed her the tracings but they needed more light to see them properly, so they walked back along the towpath to the village centre, where they slipped into the first pub for a drink to calm their nerves.

As they sat down at a table in the corner, Alex pulled out the tracings and they both looked at them. "I think it is in Welsh," she told him as she held it up to the light. "Well, the beginning is."

"Can you make sense of it?" Alex asked.

"Traphont Ddwr Pontcysyllte—Above the D—Pier10—sec 2—13 hole—14 hole," she read. "Haven't a clue," she told him as she looked at the second tracing of the emblem that Alex found on the wall above the etching. It was a shield that had a steam locomotive at the top of a bridge and he drew around it in black pen to show it up better.

"So you think that this was the Rocket?" she asked him.

"Definite," he replied. "I'll know that engine anywhere; remember our painting of the Rainhill Trials."

"Yes."

"Well, that engine was at the forefront with the other four behind it in the line."

"Yes, I can picture it now."

"Well, that was Stephenson's Rocket, which eventually won the trials."

"So do you think that this shield meant anything?"

"It's not called a shield, it's an emblem they used to be common in the nineteenth century all society had their own emblem. You know like the Masons, their emblem was black and white with three castles on it. And I know that the Engineers had a blue emblem with a yellow bridge through the centre."

"This one's got a bridge on it."

"Yes, and the Rocket, so this one must be the Stephenson's own Emblem, so I have a feeling that we are gonna see more of this emblem on our journeys."

"Well, that's the shield sorted out but what about the clue?" Julie asked. "Traphont Ddwr Pontcysyllte."

"Could be a town in Wales," Alex told her.

"Whatever it was it's written in Welsh so Wales would be a good place to start. Once we get back home, we'll type it into the computer and see what came up."

They finished their drinks, then went to the chippy for something quick to eat and then drove back to their flat above the cake shop in the village of Rishworth.

Once at home, while Julie was brewing up, Alex checked the name up on the internet. "Julie come quick, you'll never believe this," he shouted.

"What is it?" She asked. "What have you found?"

"The Traphont Ddwr Pontcysyllte is Welsh for the Pontcysyllte Aqueduct."

"The what?" she cried.

"The Pontcysyllte Aqueduct, here read what it says," he told her as he pointed to the screen.

The Pontcysyllte Aqueduct is a navigable aqueduct that carries the Llangollen Canal over the valley of the River Dee in Wrexham North East Wales. It was completed in 1805 and is the longest and highest aqueduct in Britain. When the bridge was built it linked up the villages of Froncysyllte and Trevor.

It was built by Thomas Telford and William Jessop. It is 1007 feet long, 11 feet wide and 5.25 feet deep. It consisted of a cast-iron trough supported 126 feet above the River Dee on iron arched ribs on 19 hollow masonry pillars. It opened on 26th November 1805 having taken 10 years and 47000 pounds to build.

"Above the D," Julie cried. "Above the River Dee."

"Pier 10 must mean Pillar 10 as there are 19 of them," Alex told her.

"Thirteen and 14 holes second section on pillar 10 above the river Dee."

"Bloody hell," Alex cried. "That was simple."

"Nothing that simple," Julie told him. "We don't know what the 13 and 14 holes mean yet; can we find some photos of the top of the bridge?"

Alex punched some keys and a load of photos of the bridge came up. "There that one looked good." The photo showed a view from the top of the aqueduct. It showed a walking path on one side and the canal on the other. The path had a high rail by its side, to stop people from falling, but the canal side had no rail, just a massive drop into the valley below.

"That must be the holes in question," Julie cried as she pointed to the canal wall. It looked about a foot wide and made of metal, but for some reason, there were holes in the top all along with it.

"Thirteen and 14 holes, the second section on pillar 10 above the River Dee," they both cried out together as they slapped hands together.

The next morning, while Julie was making breakfast, Alex looked over at a self-portrait of Frederick Concerve that Julie had on her wall. He smiled as he looked into Conserve's eyes and told him that he had a lot to answer for. "What are you smiling for?" Julie asked as she served him breakfast.

He walked over to the table and sat down. "I was just thinking," he replied. "How much had happened in the last year, I mean this time last year I was working in an art gallery in London and you were running the shop down below, now look at us, married, with more money than we could ever spend and eight months ago I didn't even know you existed."

"Yeah," she cried. "We may be rich but we paid a hefty price for it, both losing our best mates in the process, you with Pete dying in the car crash and me with Jay getting shot through the heart. And, why? Just because she had the same blue eyes and blonde hair as me."

Alex reached over the table and grabbed her hand, "I'm just grateful that we both managed to get through and I still can't believe that Joe and Clarence didn't take the share of the painting that we offered them."

"I suppose that they were grateful that we spoke up for them to the police, they could both be locked up now and for a very long time, they should think themselves lucky that they are free and with a hundred grand each."

Alex stroked her hand with his finger, "I guess people around here think we're strange."

"Why?" she replied.

"Well, it's common knowledge what we sold the painting for and look at us, still living above the cake shop where we first met."

"Would you rather be back in Basingstoke?"

"No," he told her. "I'm never moving back down south, I'm happy here and besides all I need is you."

"And your flash car," she replied.

"A man needs a hobby," he laughed.

"Well, at this moment our hobby is retrieving Excalibur's Gold."

"Well, what's our next move?"

"After breakfast, I'll go back online and find out all we need to know about the aqueduct and its surrounding villages, starting with Llangollen."

Julie raised her glass of freshly squeezed orange juice. "To fresh woods and pastures new," she cried.

"Sounds like poetry?" Alex replied.

Julie smiled at him, "It is, it's Milton."

Alex clicked on the internet to find out more about the village of Llangollen, which was the closest village to the aqueduct.

Llangollen- Unchanged and unspoilt Llangollen is a picturesque town that immediately captures the heart of all who visit the gateway town to the stunning countryside of North Wales. The town was established from the Iron and Bronze Age it contains everything a visitor could wish for. The ruined castle on the hill is known as the Castle of the Holy Grail and is shrouded in a history of legends. The ancient prince of Powys reputedly built it. The town church was constructed in the twelfth century and the Llangollen First Road Bridge over the River Dee was constructed in 1282. Two years later it was followed by a weekly market that still exists today.

"It seemed a nice place," Alex told her as he continued to read about it. "You won't believe this."

"What?"

"They had a re-enactment of the Rainhill Trials here in 20002, the Rainhill Trials, how about that for a coincidence."

"It can't just be a coincidence it's like we were meant to go on this quest, everything we have done has led us here."

"There seemed quite a lot of stuff going on in the village, there doesn't seem to be a month where there was nothing going on."

"See if there's any decent place to stay?" Julie asked him.

"There's a load of bed and breakfast and guest houses," he replied. "Hang on a tick, what's this. The Chainbridge Hotel."

"That looked a bit posh," Julie told him as she looked at the photo of it and read the review.

The Chainbridge Hotel is located in the magnificent Vale of Llangollen, North Wales. It is sited in a unique position literally overlooking the spectacular River Dee, with its racing white water and leaping salmon.

The Llangollen Canal begins life just a short walk away at the beautiful Horseshoe Falls which is flanked by one of the oldest roads (A5), the oldest canal' the oldest steam railway and the river Dee itself. The Chainbridge Hotel could not occupy a more uniquely beautiful location. Although standing in splendid isolation the hotel is just a short distance from the bustling centre of Llangollen.

The steam railway and the horse-drawn canal boat both travel to the hotel from the town. Or a beautiful walk along the canal towpath will lead you straight into the town centre. There is much to explore locally for all ages, the Horseshoe Pass, the Motor Museum, the working Steam Railway, Horse-drawn boat rides along the canal, plus many ancient ruins and walks to pass the time of day.

"It's not cheap," Julie told him. "But it's in an ideal location."

"See if they have a vacancy for tomorrow."

Julie managed to book them in for the next week and before they set off they checked on the internet for any information about King Arthur and the legend of him hiding under the hills in a cavern of gold. "There's quite a lot coming up about King Arthur," Alex told her.

"Anything about him hiding in a cavern until he was needed?"

"Loads and not just in Wales, it seemed that nearly every county has its own Arthur legend."

"What about him being buried in a gold mine?"

"No, nothing yet, oh hang on a sec, what's this?"

"What have you found?"

"Here," he showed her the lead line of the page that said Looking for King Arthur's gold mine in Wales?

"Click on it and see what comes up," Julie told him.

"Weird," Alex replied.

"What's weird?"

"I've clicked on it but all that comes up is a drawing of a train going through a tunnel." He clicked on it again and again but all that came up was the same drawing time after time.

At that exact moment in a luxury flat in Cardiff, a light flashed up on a computer in the office room. "Sir, Lord Gabriel," a voice rang out. "Somebody has clicked onto the page."

"The page, Joseph, what page?" a well-spoken man asked, who was sat by a desk reading some papers.

"The page, sir. The page, the page about King Arthur."

"You're joking; you mean someone's clicked onto it after all this time."

"Yes, sir."

"It could be somebody just surfing the web."

"But those exact words sir, you would have to put King Arthur's Gold Mine, that's something you just can't pick by random."

"You're right, can you find out who it was and where they are?"

Joseph smiled, "Well, you don't pay me good money just for my good looks, give me 20 minutes and I'll have a name and hopefully an address as well."

10 minutes later Joseph shouted Lord Gabriel into the office. "I've managed to trace them through their Facebook site it's a married couple an Mr and Mrs Alex Ferns, they live in a village called Rishworth, somewhere in Yorkshire."

"Can you find out more about them?" Lord Gabriel asked him.

"I've got loads here," Joseph told him. "They had just sold a painting of the Rainhill Trials for 13.6 million pounds."

"You're joking, the Rainhill Trials."

"Yeah, have you heard of the painting?"

"Yes, I have," the Lord replied. "It was painted by that scoundrel Frederick Concerve."

"The same guy who conned your ancestor out of Arthur's treasure."

"The very same guy, so the very two people who sold the Rainhill Trials painting by Concerve just happen to click on my site, that's no coincidence, they must have discovered something on the painting, a clue may be of where the Gold Mine lay. Can you trace their family trees?"

"As you wish my Lord, any second now, here it is. Alex Ferns was born in 1972 in Essex England, his father was English, his mother was German, his granddad was a POW during World War II, he was held in the Glen Mill camp in Oldham Lancashire, Parents both died in a car crash five years ago, no living descendants."

"It can't be him," the Lord replied. "Concerve or Stephenson never had kin down south, check the girls."

38

"Here you are sir, Julie Ferns-nee-Lloyd was born in Dobcross Oldham Lancashire in 1974. Father Patrick Lloyd was born in 1948 in Rochdale Lancs. Mother Jo Patterson was born in 1948 and died in 1982 in another car crash.

"Her Dad's mum was Doreen Ashcroft was born in 1922; her family owned Stott's Hall Farm, famous for being situated in the middle of the M62 Motorway that runs from Liverpool to Leeds. Now, this is interesting her great-great-grandmother Elizabeth, have a guess who her father was?"

"I can give you one of two, either Concerve or Stephenson," Lord Gabriel replied.

"Bingo," cried Joseph. "Frederick Concerve was born in 1801 in Newcastle England and died in 1870 Stott's Hall Farm Lancashire England."

"So," Lord Gabriel replied. "They are kin to Concerve; in that case, they may know something about Arthur's Mine that we don't know, well they must know something to even inquire about it, open the page."

"Beg your pardon, sir."

"Open the page and show them the maps and records that my great-great-great-grandfather Jeremiah Farthingay left behind."

"Are you sure sir, that's all we have?"

"Yeah, and look where it got us, absolutely nowhere, maybe if we dangle a bit, then maybe they will bite and we will learn a lot."

Joseph clicked on his keyboard and pressed enter, "The worms away, sir."

"Good now let's hope it dangles enough to gain their interest."

"As soon as they open the file, I can log in to their system and extract all their files without them knowing, if there's anything of interest I'll find it."

Back in Rishworth in the flat above the cake shop, Alex was startled by an alarm going off on his computer. "What the hell?" he cried.

"What is it?" Julie asked as they both raced back to the computer. "That page we clicked on," Alex told her. "The picture of the train has disappeared and look what's come up."

"It's the records of Jeremiah Farthingay," Julie replied as she eagerly clicked on the open file. "The brother of the blind guy, who Concerve mentioned in his journal." They read the file but they didn't find anything of interest in it. All it mentioned was that he searched for years in the mountains of Wales without success, it didn't even tell them the names of the mountains searched. "That was a waste of time," Julie cried as she clicked off the site.

Back in Cardiff Joseph had gained total excess into Julie's computer. "I'm in," he told Lord Gabriel. "I'll just set a trap so that we can trace their every movement online."

Lord Gabriel walked around the office with his hands behind his back. "For four generations, my family had searched the Welsh mountains for a cavern of gold," he told Joseph.

"Making a mockery of our family name, well I plan to fix that. I'll prove that the cavern exists and no more will the Farthingay name be cast as a joke. The only thing we have left is our name and I'll make damn sure that once again it will be amongst the greater families of our country. My family before me lost everything, homes, estates, money, they had it all and lost the lot through greed and snobbery,"

He stopped talking and turned around and stood to attention next to Joseph. "Do you know where I got my money, laddie?"

"Worked for it, sir," Joseph replied.

"Nay lad, did I hell, see these hands, not done a day's graft in my life, I won it, whoosh just like that. I won the lot, 18 million quid all won on the lottery, I went from being the poorest Lord in the country to whoosh overnight one very rich son-of-a-bitch."

"Sir," Joseph cried. "They have just made a booking to spend a week at the Chainbridge Hotel in Llangollen, North Wales."

"Llangollen, eh," Lord Gabriel replied as again he walked around the office stroking his chin. "Llangollen, that's in the mountains that be, if my memory was right it's quite close to the Horseshoe Pass, why would they go there? Book us in, same hotel, same day, let's see if we can keep tabs on them from a very close distance."

"Done sir, we leave in the morning," Joseph told him as he clicked enter on his lap.

Chapter Three

Pontcysyllte

Pontcysyllte Aqueduct

The next day Alex and Julie set off for Llangollen and the Chainbridge Hotel arriving just before 3:00 pm. They were checked in by the manageress, who was a cuddly woman called Stephanie, who gave them a very warm welcome. She informed them that their room wasn't ready yet but if they wanted they could wait in the bar area as they were still serving the lunchtime menu.

After having a quick bite to eat, they were informed that their room was ready so they walked up the first flight of steps to their room on the first floor which was no 15. They decided to settle in and set off for the aqueduct first thing in the morning. They got a room on the first floor and the view from their balcony was outstanding.

The first thing they noticed when they looked left was the magnificent viaduct and Victorian railway station standing supremely above the valley. Below their balcony ran the rushing waters of the River Dee. The hotel was actually on the edge of the river. To their left was the old Chainbridge that the hotel was named after. Built in the early 1800s but now not suitable for heavy traffic there was another bridge to their right that they could use to cross the river.

As they made their way down to the bar, they passed a couple of gentlemen in the hallway, there was no way that they could know that these two men were here for them. They just looked normal everyday people who would think that one was a 54-year-old Lord called Gabriel Farthingay and the other much younger taller ginger-haired man was his assistant, Joseph Arrendale, a 23-year-old who the lord had taken in when he found him living rough on the streets two years before. Joseph was so grateful for the lord taking a chance on him that he would do anything and everything the lord asked him to.

After settling in to their rooms, which were either side of Alex's, Joseph joined the Lord in the bar thereafter him making some inquires he told the lord that the couple facing them who were sat on the red chairs near the radiator were the couple they were after. The Lord decided it would be best if they didn't introduce themselves at this moment, just keep an eye on them, a very close eye.

Julie decided that she wanted to explore so she pestered Alex to join her on a walk along the side of the hotel. He really preferred to stay by the bar but after a gentle persuading, he let her have her way as usual. They walked along the steam at the front of the hotel that in fact was the beginning of the canal that went over the aqueduct some seven miles away. They then went through the swing gate that led them by the weir that was built by Telford some 250 years before. By the weir was a field where they had a lie down to sunbathe before going back to their hotel room in the early evening.

They sat on their balcony swigging on some cold beers not realising that the two men who sat on the balconies at either side of them were keeping a very close watch on them.

In the early morning, Alex and Julie set off for the aqueduct over the road bridge, closely followed by the Lord and Joseph. After taking a couple of wrong turns, they eventually found the road that took them up to the aqueduct, where they parked their car in a small car park behind some bushes just beside the walkway to the canal towpath. They walked through the bushes and onto the canal towpath that led them past the Telford inn out onto the aqueduct. They walked over to where they thought was the centre of it. "This should be quite close," Julie told him. "I've counted nine pillars below us so the clue should be right before us, can you see those holes on top of the rail over there?"

"Yes," Alex replied. "How deep did it say the water was?"

"It says that it's 5.25 feet deep," Julie told him. "How tall are you?"

"5 feet 9," he replied.

"That means that it'll come up to your mouth, I'm 5 feet 5 so it'll come up to my eyes."

"I can swim," Alex replied.

"Yeah, but look at it. It'll be freezing and you'll have to hold onto the ledge and while doing it you'll be looking over the edge at a drop of over 120 feet, remember what you were like at the viaduct. You froze and you were only about 30 feet off the ground. If you freeze here you may panic and fall over."

"That was different here I'll have a secure footing."

"Alex, will you do me a favour."

"What?"

"Turn around, put your hands on the top of the railings and look down."

"Yeah, sure I will," he replied sarcastically.

"No, bear with me, I want to try something," she told him as she put her hand on his shoulder. "Trust me."

Alex looked her in the eyes and then turned away from the canal and faced the railings. He gripped the top of the railings, took a deep breath and then looked down. "Holy shit," he cried as he quickly turned around and slid down the railings onto the floor with his head in his hands.

"See what I mean," Julie told him as she sat down beside him and threw her arms around him. "You can't do it, so I will."

"But you can't swim!" Alex cried as he looked up at her.

"It's only 5 feet I can't drown in 5 feet of water," she told him.

"5.25 feet," he replied. "And it's freezing, I can't let you do it, I'll go in."

"Are you stupid? Look at you, you can't even stand up."

"I suppose we could hire a barge," he told her as he grabbed hold of the railing and pulled himself up.

"Can you drive a barge?" she asked. "What if we didn't stop it in time, even if we went just a few feet past the clue we'd be screwed, I don't think you can reverse a barge."

"Then what about a dinghy?"

"A dinghy. A rubber dinghy," she replied. "Aren't those for kids on the seaside?"

"No," Alex told her. "I don't mean a cheap blow-a-way rubber one, I mean a hard rubber dinghy, and you can get a safe adult version from any camping or army and navy stores. We could nip into Llangollen, we passed a big camping store on the corner of the Main St. We could pick one up from there, buy a foot pump, bring it back here in the car, blow it up and float over to the mark and get the next clue."

"It could work I suppose," she replied. "Come on then what are we waiting for?"

As they walked hand in hand over the aqueduct, they didn't see the glare of the reflections of a pair of binoculars that were keeping tabs on them. As they drove off in the car, Lord Gabriel and Joseph nipped out of the bushes and onto the aqueduct. They walked over to the spot where Alex and Julie had stopped, and Alex peered over the edge.

"This was where they looked over," Lord Gabriel cried as he pointed over the railings. "What the hell were they looking at?"

As they stood there, the Lord scratching his head and his young assistant with his hands on his hips they didn't realise that they were facing the wrong way and that the clue was barely 6 feet away from them on the opposite side of the canal. They didn't have a clue where Alex and Julie had gone off to so the Lord told Joseph to hang around there while he checked back at the hotel.

A couple of hours later Alex and Julie returned to the car park, with a two man dinghy which they bought in town. But on reaching the aqueduct, they found it overran by steams of tourists and bustling barges offering trips along the canal, they had no option but to abandon their quest until the next morning. They spent a couple of hours in the village of Llangollen before having a spot of lunch in the nearby Riverside Café. They again spent the evening sat outside on the balcony watching the river rush by as the television in their room only received three channels through a lack of signal from the hotel being in the location that it was.

The next morning they set off for the aqueduct just before daybreak so as not to be disturbed by the tourists. Again they were followed by Joseph as he and the Lord had been earwigging on their conversation the night before. On parking the car up, Alex dragged the dinghy out of the boot while Julie checked that there was no sign of life in the nearby parked up barges. As Alex pumped it up by a foot pump, Julie had another look at the clue what they found in Uppermill. "Above the D, pier 10, sec 2, 13th and 14th hole," she said as she read it out loud.

"What we'll do," Alex told her. "Is we'll paddle to the spot above the river and check every hole, sign the torch down them and see if anything shows up."

On finally pumping up the dinghy and making sure that it was hard enough to take their weights, they set off for the aqueduct. As they started to walk over the aqueduct and walked past the cover of the surrounding trees, the wind started to pick up, and Alex found it very hard to keep hold of the dinghy. "The winds too strong," he told her as a sudden gust almost took the dinghy from his grasp and over the edge.

"Be careful," she replied. "We don't wanna lose it; I'm not going down there for it if you let it fall."

"I can't help it," he shouted as he dragged the rubber boat down to the floor and sat on it. "There's no shelter out there, the wind has picked up since earlier, we have no choice but to put it in the canal here and row to it."

Alex put the boat in the water and carefully got into it, but his weight wasn't enough to stop it from blowing about. "I'll have to get in as well," Julie told him. "Maybe my weight will keep it steady."

Alex managed to hold it down while Julie climbed into it. Behind the bushes stood Joseph and he phoned the Lord up to explain what they were doing. The Lord told him to keep them in sight and keep reporting back to him.

As they paddled out of the shelter of the trees, they could feel the wind picking up and attacking them from all sides. The dinghy was lifting a touch from the water but it wasn't enough to stop them from carrying on. As they floated across the aqueduct, Alex had no choice but to glance over the edge as there was no safety rail on the canal side. "Bloody hell," he cried. "I can see over the edge."

"I know," Julie shouted. "It's like we are floating in the air."

"Shit," he cried. "I'm feeling weird, I can't look."

"Turn around then and face the footpath," a sudden gust of wind almost tipped them over as he moved to face the other direction.

"Careful," she shouted. "You'll have us both in."

As he stared onto the towpath, Julie told him that they had reached the centre. "Try to spread your weight about," she told him as she reached for the side of the aqueduct. "Try to keep her steady while I have a look."

She held onto the side of the aqueduct and shone her torch down the metal holes along the top. "Nothing, nothing, nothing," she cried as she slowly pulled the dinghy from hole to hole. "There's nothing yet, just holes that you can see right through, oh, hang on a tic, what's this?"

She spotted something silver in the hole next to her. "Damn it, I can't see it properly, I'll have to get up a bit." She grabbed the rail with both hands; from where she was looking she could see the green valley and the bluish, white water of the river over 120 feet below her.

"What are you doing?" he cried. "Don't stand up, you'll fall over, the dinghy's not steady enough."

"I'll be alright," she told him as she stood up and tried to balance her weight as she peered into the hole, "There's something here, I can just reach it, just."

The next second, a sudden powerful gust of wind attacked the dinghy from behind, and with Julie stood up at the front, the wind tossed the dinghy into the air.

As Alex got dipped head first into the icy cold canal, he saw the yellow and blue dinghy blowing over the edge of the side of the aqueduct. He spluttered back to the surface. "Oh no!" he cried as he couldn't see his wife. "Julie!" he cried. "Julie."

He gripped hold of the side of the aqueduct and looked over the edge into the valley below, half fearing what he was about to see. He saw the dinghy plant itself into the branches of the row of trees by the river but he couldn't see his wife.

Down in the valley sat on the balcony of his suite Lord Gabriel was drinking an iced cold tea while talking to Joseph on the phone; he had to use a phone from reception as he couldn't receive a signal on his mobile. He jumped off his chair as Joseph told him about the yellow and blue dinghy being tossed over the edge and he franticly shouted back to Joseph to find out what had happened.

"Julie," he shouted as he nervously scoured the river and surrounding land.

"I'm here," a voice cried from behind him.

He turned around to see his beloved wife holding on to the edge of the towpath half in and out of the water. He was that surprised by the wind tossing the boat up that he didn't realise that he got tossed over Julie and that she landed behind him in the water.

He waded over to her and helped her out of the canal and then joined her on the towpath. "My God," he cried as he held her close. "I thought I lost you, I thought you went over the edge."

In the trees by the start of the aqueduct, Joseph told the lord. "That there was a slight miss-hap but everything was alright now, both were safe, wet but safe," the Lord told him to continue his watch but don't let them know he was there.

"Looks like we need another dinghy," Julie laughed as she stroked his face. Alex was shocked that she could still be so calm after what had just happened, inside he was still shaking but he couldn't let her know that so he smiled at her and gave her a kiss, then hugged her tight and told her that he loved her.

"We best get back to the hotel," he told her. "Get out of these wet clothes."

"You'll do anything to see me naked," she laughed. "But we can't leave yet, didn't you notice anything when we fell in?"

"I was too scared for your well-being to look around," he replied.

"The water, it only came up to your shoulders."

"So it did, I've just realised that."

"It must be the basin of the canal that was over 5 feet," Julie told him. "The water itself must only be 4 feet sommat, which means that even I could walk over and get the clue."

"No, you don't," he told her. "I'm not letting you back in there, I'll do it myself."

"Are you sure?"

Alex smiled at her and slid back into the water and slowly waded over to the other side. "When you look along the rail, think about me, naked in your arms don't think about the height of the bridge," she told him.

"Which hole was it?" he asked her.

"You can't miss it, all the ones before it you can see right through."

"Must be this one, I'll have to feel inside it as we have lost the torch," he replied as he reached inside with his middle finger. "Got it," he cried as he wrapped his finger around something and pulled it out of the hole.

"Don't drop it," Julie cried. "What is it?"

"It looks like some kind of hook," he replied as he held it up to the light.

"It must be to hook the clue out of the next hole," she told him. "Remember the clue, 13th and 14th hole."

Alex moved over to the next hole. "It's here," he cried. "The emblem of the Rocket is next to the hole, it's very faint but it's the same as on the wall of the viaduct." He put his middle finger into the hole and he could just feel the tip of something inside it. He tried peeping into the hole but got a glance at the massive drop into the valley. Julie saw what he was doing "Don't look down," she told him. "Look up or towards me, but whatever you do, don't look down."

He stepped back away from the edge and with an outstretched arm he dangled the hook into the hole. "Impossible," he muttered. "I need to see what I'm trying to hook if only we hadn't dropped the torch."

He continued to try to hook on to whatever was down there until suddenly he managed to snatch a hold onto it. "I think I've got it," he cried as he bravely moved back to the rail and carefully pulled the artefact to the top.

"Careful," Julie told him. "Don't drop it."

Alex looked straight ahead into the light blue sky trying desperately to blank out where he was, at least until he could get a grip on whatever it was he was pulling up. "I've got it," he shouted as he gripped a clear glass canister about the size of a test tube and waddled over to the tow-path.

"What is it?" she asked him as he handed it to her while he pulled himself out of the canal. "Don't know," he replied.

"It has a piece of paper in it," she told him. "Smash it open."

"Not here," he replied. "We'll do it in the safety of our room, knowing our luck if we broke it here the damn paper would blow away."

He put the glass canister safely into his soaking wet inside pocket and they made their way back off the aqueduct and into the warmth and safety of their car. As they drove back to the hotel, Joseph phoned Lord Gabriel and told him that they had retrieved something from the side of the canal and that they were on their way back, after which Joseph started the long walk back to the hotel himself on foot.

Gabriel ordered himself another drink and waited outside the hotel for them to arrive back. As they arrived at the hotel, Gabriel noticed the glass canister in Alex's hand. As they walked past him, he got up and followed them into the hotel desperately trying to earwig on the conversation as they walked up the flight of stairs to their room.

Once in their room, they placed the glass canister on the table and sat down. "How do we break it open?" Alex asked. "We don't want to damage the paper."

Julie looked at him and sighed, then she picked up the canister and whacked it against the edge of the sink. As the glass smashed, the paper fell onto the sink.

"Not exactly rocket science was it," she laughed as she picked up the old brown parchment.

"What does it say?" Alex asked as he noticed a puzzled look upon Julie's face.

"I don't know," she replied. "It looked like foreign writing to me; I can't make out anything on it."

"Here let me see," Alex told her as he grabbed the parchment. "You stupid get," he laughed. "It's written backwards, we need a mirror." They both dashed to the bathroom to see the reflection of the parchment in the mirror. "Hold it still," she told him as she tried to read it.

"Beyond Bosherston, through cut in cliff
75 steps down
Chapel lay
Wall of chapel as round map to r
That hid the rocket sh'd"

"Can't make out the full clue," Julie told him. "The parchment had started to disintegrate in places." She wrote down what she could make out.

"Bosherston," Alex said out loud. "Could be a town or village, never heard of it though, we need to go online again, see what comes up when we put in Bosherston." They dashed back to the table where Julie opened up her laptop to check the internet for more info.

Downstairs in their hotel room, Joseph had just returned from the aqueduct. "We need to see the clue that they brought back," Gabriel told him. "I have another little job for you."

"Whatever you wish my Lord, that's why I'm here," Joseph replied.

"I want you to go upstairs and set off the fire alarm," the Lord told him. "Once it goes off and they leave their room, I want you to break in and find the clue, don't steal it, just write down whatever it said, that would be sufficient."

"As you wish, my Lord," Joseph replied as he made his way up the stairs. He checked that no was around before he put his head against Alex's door.

Once he was sure that they were both still in their room, he broke the glass on the fire alarm and then set it off. He wasn't expecting them to exit their room so quick; he was almost seen as he pressed himself against the corner near their room. Once he was sure that everyone had left the hotel, he went back to his room and jumped over the railings of his balcony over onto Alex's. He didn't even have to break into the room because Julie had left the door wide open so he quickly started to search.

Outside in the car park, Alex was stood next to Julie blowing on his hands. "Bloody hell, it's cold out here," he told her.

"Should have got your coat," she replied. "I managed to grab mine."

"I didn't think did I, I thought that the place was on fire."

"I can't smell anything nor see any smoke, must be a faulty alarm or sommat," she replied.

"See that guy over there," Alex whispered into her ear. "The guy with the small round glasses and jet black hair."

"Yes," she replied. "He was sat behind us at breakfast this morning, what about him?"

"Well, you know that young tall ginger lad he was with."

"Yes."

"Well, I can't be positive but I'm sure that I saw him behind us on the stairs when we were rushing out of the hotel."

"How come he's not here then?"

"Exactly and I'm sure that the older one keeps looking at us, look at him, he keeps looking at his watch and then giving us a sly glance out the corner of his eye, there did you see it?"

Julie nodded and then brushed into his shoulder and pointed her head to the other side of the hotel where Joseph had just walked around. They looked to the Lord who stared towards Joseph who nodded back to him. At that moment, the owner of the hotel apologised to all the guests and told them all that it was safe to go back inside now.

Once back in their room, the Lord asked Joseph what he had found. Joseph told him that he couldn't find the clue but he did find a notebook that looked as if someone had been writing in it. He handed the Lord the notebook. Joseph then joined Gabriel at the table as he rubbed a pencil over the impression on the paper. The Lord realised straight away that it was the clue and he had an idea what it meant.

"As a kid, my father used to send me to a private school in Hundleton South Wales," the Lord told his young assistant.

"On the coast down, there was a town called Bosherston. And if I'm not mistaken there was a tiny chapel by the seafront. The only way to get to it was through a cutting in the cliffs down loads of steps. I can't remember the name of the chapel but it must be the one in the clue."

"Sir," Joseph replied. "I don't think that the couple had figured out the clue yet, otherwise why would they still be here?"

"Pack the bags," the Lord told him. "It won't take them long, not if they go on the internet, blasted invention, anything could be tracked down on that infernal device, still we have the upper hand and I'm not going to lose it."

In the room above them, Alex was searching for his notebook. "I'm sure I put it down here, I had it in my hand when the fire alarm went off I'm sure of it."

"Speaking about the fire alarm," Julie replied as she looked out of their room door. "Isn't that, that man and his mate rushing out of the hotel with their bags under the arms?"

Alex suddenly had a nasty thought and ran down the hallway to the fire exit at the end that overlooked the car park. "Nice car," he said as he watched them get into a silver vintage E-Type Jaguar. He walked back to the room, "I wonder where they are going in such a hurry?" He looked into Julie's face and then to the table. "No," he cried. "They couldn't have, no one knows."

"No one knows what?" Julie asked him.

"About our quest, no one knows, but then again I swear he was behind us on the stairs, but he never came out."

"Who didn't?" Julie asked. "What are you babbling on about?"

"That young lad with the man with black hair, he was I'm sure, he was behind me and now my notebook has vanished and they are rushing off, they must know and more than that they must know where the clue leads to."

"But you have the clue in your wallet."

"Remember the first clue by the viaduct, I traced it, if they had my notebook they could have traced over the writing."

"Shit, you're right, he was watching us, we both knew that," Julie cried. "And we saw the young lad nod to him when he appeared."

"He was telling him that he had the notebook, shit, we need to find out where the next clue is, and quick." Julie clicked online and typed in Bosherston. "While you do that I'll go down and find out who they were?"

"They won't tell you," Julie told him. "It's hotel policy not to give out private details."

"Well," Alex replied. "How can we find out who they were?"

"I'll go down and ask," Julie told him as she got up from her seat.

"Like they'll tell you."

"Trust me, I'm a woman and a woman can make anyone talk, you check Bosherston out and I'll go down to reception."

As Alex waited for his laptop to log online, Julie dashed down to reception. "Excuse me," she cried to the young lad on reception.

"Yes, mam," the young lad replied. "How may I be of help?"

"Do you know that man who had just checked out, the black-haired guy who was with the other young man?"

"Lord Gabriel," the receptionist replied. "What about him?"

"Well, it's just that I've got a bet going with my partner," Julie told him. "He thinks that they were a couple, and I think not."

The receptionist laughed and shook his head. "Oh no," he replied. "They were not gay, that was Lord Gabriel Farthingay and his personal assistant Mr Arrendale, and no they are not gay."

"A Lord," Julie replied. "And we thought him to be gay. Lord Farthingay now that was interesting," she thanked him for his time before dashing up to tell Alex about the Lord.

"You won't believe this," she cried as she burst into the room.

Alex couldn't believe it when she told him who their stalker was. He clicked off the page he was logged on to and typed in Lord Gabriel Farthingay and waited for the results to come up.

After a couple of minutes, about 10 pages cropped up and Alex clicked onto the first page. "Gabriel Farthingay, aged 44," he read out loud as the page came up. "Both parents dead, plane crash in the late 1980s. Gabriel was committed after their deaths for trying to kill himself.

"He again got committed for burning down a family home when he was 30 and committed again at the age of 35 for trying to shoot a gardener who cut down his ivy after mistaking it for weeds. The family had lost all its fortune and estates, Gabriel himself was totally skint until he won a fortune on the lottery six years ago."

"Look at the pictures of him," Julie cried as she pointed to photographs of the Lord. "Look closely, the picture from 1998 he had blond curly hair, a long chin and a broken nose, compare it with the one from last year. Short dark hair and he has had a nose job and a new chin, obviously he didn't like who he was."

"Committed three times," Alex told her. "Once for shooting somebody, he sounds like a total nut job, we best play it safe, he knows about us, but he doesn't know that we are onto him yet."

"What does he want though?" Julie asked.

"Obviously, that page we clicked onto about Arthur's Gold Mine was the work of him," Alex told her. "He's rich, very rich, so it can't be the money he's after."

"Maybe he's like us," Julie replied. "He may be after it for his family's sake, look at what it said about his family, they lost everything, maybe he's trying to get his estates back or something."

"Whatever he was after," Alex told her. "If he was after clearing his family's name then why didn't he reveal himself instead of breaking into our room and stealing from us, I still think we need to find the next clue before him," Alex clicked off the Lord's page and typed in Bosherston.

"Bosherston," Alex cried as it came up on a map. "It's in South Wales, in Pembrokeshire, a small town on the coast."

"Anything about a small chapel?" Julie asked.

"Hang on," he told her as he typed in Chapel by the sea. "Here, St Govan's Chapel, St Govan's Head, Grade 1 listed ancient monument built between the sixth and twelfth centuries."

"St Govan's head," Julie said as she bit her finger. "Why does that sound familiar? I remember it was a poem my mother used to tell me, now how did it go, ha, I've got it."

St Govan

St Govan, he built him a cell
By the side of the Pembroke sea
And there, as the crannied sea-gulls dwell
In a tiny, secret citadel
He sighed for eternity

St Govan, he built him a cell
Between the wild sky and the sea
Where the sunsets redden the rolling swell
And brooding splendour has thrown her spell

On valley and moorland lea

St Govan still lies in his cell
But his soul, long since is free
And one may wonder- and who can tell-
If good St Govan likes heaven as well
As his cell by that sounding sea?

"Where did that come from?" Alex asked as he looked at his wife with a smile on his face.

"I don't know," she replied. "A memory that had long since been locked away, as soon as I heard the name St Govan's it came into my head, it was written by A.G. Prys-Jones, way before I was born, my mother used to own a book by the poet, it was handed down by her mother, I had it myself but it got lost in transit over the years, anyway enough about me what does it say about the chapel?"

"It's coming up now," Alex told her. "Signals not very good here, connections very slow. St Govan's chapel, here it is."

St Govan's Chapel—Out on the cliffs of the spectacular Pembrokeshire National Park, five miles or so south of Pembroke and a mile beyond the village of Bosherston lay the picturesque sixth century chapel of St Govan.

To enter the chapel you must descend a long flight of steps that carry you through the cliffs and down to the chapel. The chapel is simply constructed, having just a nave that measures approximately 5.3 m by 3.8 m.

At the east end of the chapel is a stone altar and steps that lead to a small cell that was formed in the rock. The south wall contains a piscine, a small aperture and the main window.

The north wall is plain except for the entrance and a small recess or shelf. The west wall has a circle in the rough plastering high up and to the right of the centre, within the circle, there was an inscription, but all that was visible now are what looks like a 6 and a 0.

Experts say that these are the only original marks on the walls. The west wall also has a small window and a doorway leading out to the rocks below and to a roughly built well. Experts agree that the building was at least as old as the eleventh century with some claiming it as early as the 6th. Outside the chapel is a large rock boulder known as the Bell Rock.

Legend is that St Govan was given a silver bell which was stolen by pirates from its bell tower. St Govan prayed for its return and angels retrieved it and placed it inside a rock where it would be safe. St Govan used to tap the rock that gave a note thousand times stronger than the original bell.

"Well, that sounds like the right place," Alex told her. "It even mentioned the cut through the cliff, the steps and even circle on the wall."

"Yes," Julie replied. "But it also mentioned that there was only a 6 and a 0 in the circle, nothing else was original."

"You're not thinking right are you?" Alex told her. "Original, meaning sixth or eleventh century, we are looking for a clue from the 19th remember."

"God you're right, how thick am I, don't answer that, how long will it take us to get there?"

Alex clicked onto the internet mapping service but his connection failed so he reached for his road map. "We are here," he told her as he pointed to Llangollen on the map,

"We will go over to the A5 follow it down to Oswestry then get onto the A483 follow it all the way down to Llandovery, wherever that is? Then get onto the A40 follow that all the way to Haverfordwest then take the A4076 to Pembroke and then the B4319 to the seafront. In short, it looks like we have to drive all the way through central Wales and some of these roads go on and on for miles through the mountains."

"Can't we just cut towards Shrewsbury and get onto the M6?" Julie asked as she pointed towards the nearest motorway.

"We could, but look," Alex told her as he moved his finger towards the M6. "It would take us over an hour to get onto it, even if you save time on the motorway as soon as you get back into Wales there is nothing but A roads, and believe me, the A470 down there goes for miles, we don't have to worry about him finding the clue tonight anyway it's almost half one now, it'll be dark by the time he gets there, as long as we are there for first light.

"If we sleep in the car by the entrance then we will be first to the chapel in the morning, I can't see a Lord slumming it in a car and there doesn't seem to be anywhere else closer than the village for him to sleep in."

Chapter Four

St Govan's Chapel

St Govans Chapel

Alex paid the bill while Julie packed the bags, and by 2:00 pm, they were on their way to South Wales. The Lord had a lead of about an hour but he was heading towards the motorway. "Sir," Joseph cried. "We are going the wrong way; the satnav is directing us towards the A5 to Shrewsbury we should be going the other way."

"Must be quicker over the motorway," the Lord replied. "The satnav will always pick the quickest route, forget about the road map and trust it."

Joseph looked at his road map. "I guess you're right," he replied. "The A5 turns into the M54, and then it's the M5, M6, M48 and M4. Motorways all the way until Llanelli and from there it looked about half an hour to the Chapel, I would say about five hours drive in all."

"As long as we get there before dark, I want to be long gone by the time those two show up later in the week," the Lord replied. "Shit, what does he want?"

The Lord noticed a blue flashing light in his rear-view mirror. It was a police car and it was pulling him over for speeding. The policeman walked around the Lord's gleaming silver E-Type Jaguar admiring it before smiling at the Lord and asking him if he was in a rush. After being held up for over 20 minutes, the Lord set upon his journey, with the added bonus of a sixty pounds fine and three more points on his license.

About an hour later they reached the M54 motorway that led them to the M6. As soon as they got near Birmingham on the M6, the traffic ahead started to slow to a snail's pace and they saw a sign warning them about long delays between junctions 10 and 8 of the motorway.

Alex and Julie meanwhile were making good headway, there seemed to be no traffic about the way they had chosen and they reached Welshpool in less than an hour to join onto the A483. The delays on the M6 had cost the Lord over an hour of driving time and he was becoming quite annoyed. Finally, the traffic started flowing again only for it to come to a halt as soon as they moved onto the M5 "Damn it," the Lord cried as he saw another sign warning of more long delays between junctions 4 and 6 of that motorway.

"We had hardly moved in the last hour," Joseph cried as they lost another hour of their day stuck in the traffic jam that was caused by an accident near Gloucester.

Eventually, they got going and within another hour they crossed the Severn Bridge into Wales, where they met up with more delayed traffic on the M4 near Cardiff. "Damn it," the Lord cried. "We'll never get there at this rate."

Alex and Julie were now in South Wales themselves. They had just turned onto the A40 and were making good time. "Something's wrong," Julie cried as they passed the village of Trecastle. "I can't see this place on the map; pull in at this lay-by so I can find out where we are."

Alex pulled into the lay-by and parked up by a burger van while Julie checked the map. "That's the problem," she told him. "We turned left onto the A40 we should have turned right."

They decided to make use of the burger van because they didn't have a clue how much longer the journey was going to take. While Alex ordered them both a meal and a drink Julie planned the route ahead.

It was now almost 8:00 pm, and the night was slowly catching them up. "Damn it," Lord Gabriel cried as he punched the dashboard. "It'll be too bloody dark now when we arrive, we'll have to check in to a guest house for the night when we get to Bosherston, bloody satnav, who said that they made your journey easier, we would have been bloody quicker walking."

They arrived in Bosherston at 9:15 pm and soon found a bed for the night in a local public house. Alex and Julie arrived in the village about half an hour later but drove straight to the rifle range that overlooked the edge of the cliff where the chapel was situated. Alex quietly opened the gates so that they could drive through the range and park overlooking the cliff. "Pity we lost the torch," Alex told her. "If we still had it, then we could have found the clue right now, it'll be too dangerous to try to walk through the cliffs in the dark."

Julie agreed with him and decided it best to have a kip and wait for daybreak.

Alex tried to reverse the car away from the edge but the engine cut. "What happened?" Julie asked.

"You're not going to believe this but we're out of petrol."

"You're joking."

"I wish I were, but it doesn't matter, we passed a petrol station about a mile up the road, in the morning I'll jog up and bring some back."

Meanwhile, after settling into their rooms, Gabriel and Joseph had met up in the bar and were having a quiet drink. "I know that you think that we are wasting our time and that I'm an old fool with too much money," Gabriel told his young assistant.

"No, sir," Joseph replied. "I would never say that."

"No, maybe not old but you think I'm foolish."

"I would never say that sir, you know I won't."

"No, you haven't lad and you never will, but you must think it, and you'll be a fool not to, but believe in me lad and your name will go down in history I promise you that."

"I do believe in you sir, but surely there must be an easier way of finding the mountain than by following all these stupid clues?"

The Lord looked at him and smiled, "Over the past five years, I have tried everything I know to locate the mountain, God knows how much money I wasted on all the new contraptions, all the geological surveys, for Christ sake I even paid for a satellite survey of all the Welsh mountains and still found nothing.

"I've had dozens of qualified men, teachers, professors, men with brains to shame both of us to personal search through the mountains with all the hi-tech stuff money could afford, they geo-fizzed every God damn yard and still found nothing something about their equipment couldn't see through the clay, so if the clues work then I'd be damn stupid not to follow them."

"But how can you have trust in the clues if you hate the men who left them?" Joseph asked as the Lord took a sip of his beer.

"Stephenson was no fool, I'd give him that," Gabriel replied. "He was an intelligent man, he knew his stuff and he must have realised that man would progress significantly in the years after his death. He had the means and the manpower, for Christ sake he could have built a railway station over the entrance without any of the workers knowing.

"I know that you're thinking that the gold mine could just be a myth and may not exist, but I can't allow myself to think that way. My ancestor found something and I plan to find out what.

"Ever since that fateful day all those years ago my family have been searching for it, it has destroyed our family, our name is rubbished when two centuries ago it was up there with the best, I have to prove it exists, not for me but for my name and all my family who had been ridiculed before me." Gabriel lifted up his glass. "To my family," he toasted.

"People think I'm mad," he told Joseph. "Do you think I'm mad?"

Joseph laughed, "Eccentric maybe, but not mad sir."

"Nay lad," Gabriel replied. "You'd be wrong, as Tony Perkins said in Psycho; everyone goes a little mad sometimes. And I've had my dark times lad, believe me, really dark and bad times, more than a normal person's share, but hopefully, those times are well and truly behind me."

He lifted up his glass again, "Here's to the future and may it be kind to us. We never really spoke about your family, did we? You know everything about me but your life before me is still a mystery to me."

"My life before you was over, there's nothing to tell, no family, no friends nothing, you found me on the streets and that was my life," Joseph replied as he put his glass down on the table.

"Surely there must have been a girl, more than one I reckon?" Gabriel asked.

"Sir," Joseph told him. "Look at me, what do you see?"

"A good looking lad in his early 20s, young strong," Gabriel replied.

"I'm not good looking, I'm a freak," Joseph told him.

"You're not a freak, who would call you a freak?"

"Everyone, back in my home village of Eldersfield in Gloucestershire," Joseph replied as he took a big gulp from his glass. "I never spoke you see, I was quiet, very shy I never knew what to say to people and whenever anyone would look at me I would turn away from them, I mean look at me I've been this big since my early teens, 6 feet 4 with bright orange hair, people would call me names at school, called me a freak, with every incident, I would back off further into my shell, my own little world.

"Then one day a young girl went missing and everyone pointed a finger at me. Just because I'm quiet it doesn't make me a freak. Anyway I got pulled in by the cops, they couldn't prove anything so they had to release me, but that didn't stop people from talking, staring. Then one night I got jumped by a group of lads in the village centre.

"People stood by and watched as they battered me to a pulp. People stood by and cheered as I got kicked and punched to the floor. They clapped as every punch hit home, cheered and shouted kill the paedo bastard. I knew I was innocent, but I was guilty by association, the cops pulled me in so I must have been guilty."

"What happened?" Gabriel asked.

"As soon as I got out of the hospital, I legged it, I mean I had no choice, even my father thought I had done it, how could I live in a village where everyone thought me to be a child killer, I ran and ran and ran, living on the street for months and that's where you found me, you didn't treat me like a freak you treated me as a human being and I'd never had that for years, you didn't judge me, and for that, you earned my undying respect."

"I sensed something in you lad," Gabriel told him as he threw his arm around his young assistant. "I sensed you to be pure-hearted."

"For the first time in my life sir, I feel like I belong, you don't make me feel like a freak and I actually feel like I was born to serve you," Joseph stood up and hugged the Lord.

"That's enough son," Gabriel told him as he sat Joseph back into his seat. "It can't be good for your image to be seen hugging a man old enough to be your father, people will think we are a couple."

They both looked to the next table and saw the couple sat down staring at them. They both started to laugh and the Lord raised his glass. "To us," he cried. "And bugger the rest."

The next morning, Alex and Julie were awoken by the sound of tapping on the roof of the car. "What's that," a weary Alex cried as he shot his head up off Julie's chest.

"It's nothing," Julie replied as she wiped the sleep from her eyes. "It's raining, that's all."

"More like a bloody thundershower, what time is it?"

"8 o'clock," she told him.

"Night-time or day?"

"It's morning, you dopey get," she replied.

"Well, it bloody looked like night, look at the sky, how dark it is. It's normally light by now in spring."

The next second, they were shocked by the sight of a lightning bolt that struck the tree about twenty feet away from the car. "I don't think it's safe to remain here," Alex told her. "If it had hit the car we'd be dead by now, grab your coat and let's run down the path, we could shelter in the chapel, we'd be safe there."

They grabbed their coats and huddled together as they braved the atrocious weather. As they rushed down the darkened path through the cliffs and down the steps, Alex slipped and tumbled down a few steps and onto the rocky grass verge and slid into the rocks below. "Are you all right?" Julie screamed as she ran down the remaining steps to where her husband lay curled up against a rock.

Luckily, he was only shaken and she helped him up and into the dryness of the old chapel.

Once Alex had recovered his composure, they pulled out the clue they found on the aqueduct

Beyond Bosherston
through cut in cliff,
75 steps down,
chapel lay,
wall of chapel as round map to r
that hid the rocket sh'd.

"We've gone down the steps and into the chapel," Alex told her. "Now what wall would the circle be on?"

"Can't see anything," Julie replied. "It's still too dark, we'll have to wait until the weather clears and the sun comes out, then we'll have the light required."

Julie sat on the steps up to a small cell, while Alex sat beside her on what looked like an old altar. After what seemed like hours but was only about 45 minutes, the storm clouds blew over and the sun began to creep out. As the sunlight lit the chapel by way of the windows and doorway, they could now see around them. The altar was on the east wall of the chapel.

The south wall contained a piscina, a small aperture and the main window. The north wall was plain except for the entrance and a small shelf while on the west wall they found the circle in the rough plastering, high up and to the right of centre. Within the circle were the remains of an inscription but all they could make out was what looked like a 6 and an 0, everything else on the wall was modern graffiti left by the more ignorant of the common tourists.

"I can't understand it," Julie cried. "There must be more than this; there doesn't seem much room in the circle for anything else."

"Give me a leg up," Alex told her. "There's something under the 6 and 0."

Julie gave him a leg up and watched as Alex scraped away years of debris from beneath the numbers. "Have you found something?" she asked him.

"Something," he replied. "I can make out another number below these, I'm sure it's a two, yes I'm positive it's a two."

"A 6, a 0 and a 2," Julie said as Alex dropped to the floor. "What the hell did that mean, 602 yards out of the chapel under the rock it led you to, do you think?"

"It's in that order," Alex replied. "I guess it's worth a shot."

They walked out of the chapel and started to walk down the hill until they realised that there weren't any rocks that way and every other way they tried there were no rocks anywhere that matched 602 yards.

"What the hell can 602 mean?" Alex said as he stood by the edge of the rocky bay and stared towards a rock formation about a mile down the coast that led out into the sea.

"You're joking me!" he cried out as he looked over to the cliff and started to move his finger about in the air tracing the shape of the rock formation. "Pass me a pen and paper quick," he cried.

"What is it? What have you found?" she replied as she searched in her bag for a pen.

"The camera will do," he told her as he walked to the water's edge.

She gave him the digital camera and he zoomed in to the cliff and took a photo, then he ran off towards the chapel. "Quick follow me," he cried as he ran over the rocks. "You'll never believe this."

"What have you found?" she asked him again as they entered the chapel.

"Maybe nothing, maybe a lot," he replied as he made his way to the wall that held the circle in it. He zoomed the camera to the circle in the rough plastering and then slowly pulled the camera down the wall underneath. "I don't believe it, how good am I."

"Do you know what it means?" she asked him again.

"I do now," he replied with a beam across his face. "Follow me."

She looked at him with a puzzled upon her face as again he raced out of the chapel and down to the rocky bay. "Look at that big cliff going out to the sea," he told her as he pointed across.

"That's St Govan's head," she told him. "What about it?"

"Look what was underneath the circle," he replied as he showed her the picture on the camera. "Can you see it? It's a carving off that cliff."

"Blimey you're right," she replied as she held the camera up to the cliff. "I've got it, I know the clue, it wasn't a 6, a 0 and a 2, it must be a G and an O and a 2, meaning GO 2 ROCK THAT HID THE ROCKET SHIELD, that rock because if you look closer there's a mark in the carving that doesn't match up and that mark was in the place of that cave over there."

"So," Alex cried as he interrupted her. "In that cave lies the mark of the Rocket, the emblem that was on the other clues, so if we find the emblem then we would find the next clue."

"What are we waiting for then?" she replied as she started her way across the rocky beach. "We're lucky that the tides had just gone out," he told her as he joined her. "There's no way to reach it if is in."

Lord Gabriel and Joseph had just finished their breakfast and were on their way to the chapel. "I don't believe it, sir," Joseph cried as he spotted Alex's red Jaguar parked on the edge of the cliff as they walked through the firing range towards it.

"Damn it," Gabriel shouted. "That was definitely their car, how the hell did they beat us to it."

"Sir I can see them down on the shore, they seemed to be heading for that cliff," Joseph told him.

St Govans Head

"Damn it," the lord shouted. "They mustn't have found the clue yet, never mind young lad, they may get the clue but there's no way that they will be able to use it, give us a hand."

"What have you in mind, sir?" Joseph asked as he followed Gabriel towards the car.

Down below Alex and Julie had reached the cave by the bottom of St Govan's head and were scouting the walls for the emblem. "It'll be on the west wall," Alex told her. "About there."

"It wouldn't be at a reachable height, look at the tide marks on the wall they must go almost to the top."

"Not quite," Alex told her as he pointed to the very top of the wall. "There's about a foot up there where the tide has never reached." He pointed the camera up and zoomed into and across the wall until finally catching sight of a shield carved into the rock. "I've got it," he cried. "There is an emblem but it's worn away but I can make out the bridge at the top of it."

"Anything else?" she asked.

"Yes, there's a ledge just above it, looked about 6 inches long."

"How the hell do we reach it?" Julie asked. "We can't bring a ladder all the way down here, besides we wouldn't fit one in the car, I mean it may look good but it wasn't actually a car for packing stuff into it was it."

"I don't care what you say about my car, I love it and we're keeping it," Alex replied. "Now I've got an idea how we can reach the ledge, if you look up there it's still dripping so that means that the last tide reached all the way, the tides going out now so if we come back in about 10 hours' time, the tide will be back in and I could swim up to the ledge."

Julie shook her head. "I'm not letting you do that. Are you stupid?" she cried. "The tide will be at full strength, you wouldn't last two minutes in there with it, it'll drag you out and you'll drown."

"I've already thought about that," Alex replied. "We need to bring back a long thick rope with us, and before you open your mouth it will fit in the car. If we bring a rope, I'll tie it around me and then you could tie it around that rock up there, it's well away from the tide, you'll be safe and then I'll jump in, swim to the ledge and get the clue, what could go wrong?"

"I guess I can't talk you out of this," she replied as she smiled at him. "You could still drown, you know."

"Not with my beautiful young bride holding the reigns, I trust you, my love, and don't worry; I will be safe."

"I still don't like it."

"The only way, my darling, but first, we need to find us somewhere where we can get some kip, I don't know about you but I hardly got a wink last night, what with the wind and all the other weird noises."

"You just want my body to admit it," she laughed.

"I would never turn down such a delicious treat but today it's the sleep we need," he replied as he threw his arm around her shoulder and led her over the rocky beach back towards the chapel.

"You got to be chuffing joking!" Alex cried as he looked up past the chapel.

"What's up," Julie asked. "What is it?"

Alex couldn't speak he could only point to the top of the cliff with his finger.

"Isn't that your car rolling down the cliff?" she replied as she held her hand over her mouth in shock.

At the top of the cliff, the Lord and Joseph looked down as the car smashed into the rocks below "Damn it," Gabriel cried. "I thought the damn thing would have blown up, I love a good fire."

"Sir," Joseph whispered. "We'd best get away from here before anyone sees us."

Alex and Julie ran over the rocky beach to where the car came to rest "Look at her," Alex cried. "How the hell did she fall, the handbrake was on I'm sure."

"Good job we were out of fuel," Julie replied. "Otherwise it would be," she looked at her husband's face. "She would have exploded by now, come on we best get our bags." As Julie climbed over the rocks to pick their bags up that had been thrown onto the rocks as the car broke up. Alex was down on his knees with his head in his hands in shock. Julie got both their bags and walked back over to her husband, and for some unknown reason, she started to laugh.

"I'm glad you find it funny," he growled at her.

"I'm sorry, my love. I really am, but the look on your face as it rolled down the cliff, my God I wish I had a camera on you."

"It's not funny, I loved that car."

"Could have been worse," she told him.

"How?" he cried. "How could it have been any worse?"

"Well, my Prince, it could have rolled over the edge in the night while we slept."

"My God!" he cried. "You're right, I could have killed you."

"Us," she replied. "You could have killed us."

He grabbed hold of her and held her tight to him "If I lost you, I couldn't carry on, you're my life," he whispered as he kissed her forehead. She just smiled at him and kissed him on the lips and then they started the long tiring walk up the old steps to the top of the cliffs where their car had fallen from.

"That's funny," Alex cried as he spotted broken glass on the floor. "Windows don't smash before the car hits the ground, somebody broke it. Somebody pushed it over on purpose."

"Who?" Julie asked. "And why?"

"There's only one person who could gain from this."

"Lord Farthingay."

"Yes, he must have seen us below and thought that we had the clue, he must have thought that the only way to stop us was to get shut off our transportation."

"The sneaky bastard," Julie cried.

"Yes, but he doesn't know us, does he?" Alex replied. "This won't hold us up, there was nothing we could do until this evening anyway, and now we won't have to waste time walking to the bloody petrol station for petrol for her."

"But we still need to sleep and find some rope."

"We passed a pub couple of miles down the road; hopefully, we can get a room there," Alex grabbed her hand and they walked over the driving range and towards the road. What they didn't know was that Gabriel and Joseph were parked up in a cut off waiting for them to go by. Once they had passed, the Lord and Joseph drove back to the rifle range and made their way down to the chapel. They also mistook the meaning of the clue, and after checking all the rocks, they gave up, and with no other means of figuring the clue out, they decided to head back to town and try to find Alex and Julie.

"They walked off that way my Lord," Joseph told him as they got back into their car.

"We passed a pub up there," Gabriel replied. "So no guessing where they have headed to, we'll go to the pub ourselves and we'll book in also and make sure that we keep them in sight at all times." Gabriel dropped Joseph off at the public house to book them in while he went back to where they stayed the night before to pick up their stuff.

After booking in, Joseph soon discovered what room Alex was in by checking the register as he signed in and by luck he was in the room next to theirs while Gabriel was in a room above them.

Gabriel returned within the hour to find Joseph having a smoke in the beer garden round the back of the pub. Joseph informed him that he hadn't seen them but that they were still in their room and that he left word with the guy on the desk to tell him when they leave the hotel. The next minute, that very same guy was waving at Joseph through the window "If you excuse me, my Lord, I think I've got some more news for you," Joseph told him as he got up off his seat and walked over to the window.

After an exchange of a few notes, Joseph came back smiling "They have just ordered a taxi to take them to Bosherston, he says they were asking him where they could buy a car from."

"Then if we set off now, we'll be in the village before them and there weren't that many places where you could buy a car from," Gabriel replied.

"Just that small place near the pub we stayed at," Joseph told him.

"Well, what we'll do," Gabriel replied. "Is park facing the car yard and make sure we note what car they buy and what the number plate was, we have come too far now to lose it at this late stage."

"But sir," Joseph told him. "What if this clue just leads us to another and then another, we could be following them for months from one side of the country to another."

"I don't think so, if I'm right then there will be six or seven clues and then whoosh the big revelation, don't ask me how I know, I just have this feeling that we are very close, very close indeed and no one was going to get in my way, not this time."

"Sir, I don't mind helping you with anything but you're not gonna get into any rough stuff are you, I mean I'm no killer."

Gabriel smiled towards his young assistant and then burst out laughing "Joseph my boy," he cried. "I don't mean that, my God I've never raised my hands to a woman in my life, when I said I'd do anything I didn't mean I'd kill for the treasure, my God my young friend I only mean to stop them from finding it before me, in fact, if I knew that I could trust them, then I would gladly join forces with them, but in this life, trust must be earned not given."

After waiting outside the car yard for about an hour, they saw Alex and Julie get out of a taxi and walk into the yard. Less than an hour later they saw them leave driving a red Vauxhall Corsa. Gabriel and Joseph followed them into the centre of the village and watched while Alex and Julie parked up by an outdoor pursuit shop.

"What are they up to?" Gabriel asked as he saw them return back to their new car with what looked like a big stretch of strong rope on a coil. "The clever bleeders must have discovered what the clue meant and where it led to," he told Joseph as he started up the car and followed them back to the pub where they were staying.

Later in the evening Alex and Julie set off to catch the late tide. With them, they took the coil of rope and a couple of new torches. They had an inkling that Gabriel and Joseph were around but that didn't distract them from going after the clue.

When they reached the chapel they hit upon their first snag for the tide was already in and had washed away their path along the beach towards St. Govan's Head. They had to walk back up the 70 odd steps to the top of the cliffs and find another way to St. Govan's Head.

They found a gap in the fence of the rifle range about half a mile further down the shore. They climbed through the fence and found a path through the cliffs that led them along the top of the cliff itself. What they didn't see was Gabriel and Joseph sneaking along behind them.

"We could go for it from here," Julie told Alex as they looked over the edge into the wild raging sea beneath them. "Tie the rope around you and I'll lower you down."

"Are you crazy?" Alex cried. "If I go in here, the strength of the tide may drag me anywhere and we have nowhere to tie the rope to here, if you try to hold my weight, it may pull you in, I'm not having that, we'll go down there," he told her as he pointed to some rocks by the side of the Head.

"There are plenty of rocks down there that we could tie it to plus there is a life ring on that pole we'll borrow that, tie the rope to it and I'll wear it, then you'll know that I won't drown."

"Where are they going?" Joseph asked as they watched them make their way carefully down the side of the cliff towards the rocks.

"The clue must be in that cave by the bottom," Gabriel replied. "That's why they brought the rope, sooner them than us, it's gonna be cold in there."

At the bottom, Alex picked up the life ring and tied the rope to it, very tight, and then he wrapped the rope around a tall thin rock and tied it, again very tight. "You'll be safe here," he told Julie as he kissed her on the lips. "The tide shouldn't reach up here."

"Take care, my love," Julie shouted as he waded into the oncoming tide. "Any problems come straight out."

Alex smiled at her and then turned around to face the cave or what he could see of it for it was almost hidden by the rising waters of the ravaging Celtic Sea.

"What the hell am I doing?" he asked himself as the water soon hit his chin.

He took a deep breath and started to swim towards the top. It was very hard going, very hard. He thought himself to be a very good swimmer but in these waters being a good swimmer wasn't enough. For every stroke forward, he managed the savage waters that drove him back three.

He only had to swim about 20 feet, but it seemed like he was swimming for miles until eventually, he reached the cave through the chopping waters. But even when he got there the waters pushed him first backwards and then dragged him forward and way past the cave and out past the safety of the cliff and into the open sea.

Only the length of the rope stopped him from being sucked away into never land, but as he desperately tried to pull himself back along the rope a sudden gust of waves pushed the life ring over his head and away from him.

Julie watched in horror as wave after wave buffeted Alex tossing him up and across the cold waters. Just as the undercurrent was about to drag him under he managed to grab a hold of the life ring and wrapped his arm around it and gripped it tight between his shoulder and his chest.

Julie sighed with relief as she saw him fumble the ring over his head, but what she didn't see was the rope uncoiling itself from around the rock. By the time she noticed, it was too late for the next big wave dragged Alex back out into the open sea and the rope left the rock.

She dived onto the rope and wrapped it around her wrist and dug her heels into the rock to stop herself from sliding forward. She held on with all her might to save her beloved husband from being swept to his death, but her hands were becoming sweaty and the rope started to slip through her hands.

Alex didn't know the battle that Julie was facing in keeping a grip on the rope for he had his own battle for life with the ravaging waters of the Celtic Sea to worry about. Julie cried out in agony as the rope slipped from her grasp.

"Hang on love!" a voice cried out from behind her. "We're coming." It was Gabriel and Joseph; they had been watching from above and realised that Alex was in mortal danger.

Joseph waded into the frightening waters and grabbed the rope, wrapping it around his chest he battled to make his way back to the safety of the rocky shore.

"I'm here lad," Gabriel shouted as he waded in to help his young assistant. With Gabriel also gripping the rope and pulling it, they eventually managed to drag Alex from the jaws of death and onto the safety of the rocks.

"Mind out love," Joseph cried as he rushed to Alex's side. "I know first aid."

Luckily Alex didn't need the kiss of life from his young saviour and he quickly came around. As he lay on the rocks with Gabriel's jacket over him, Alex asked the Lord "Why did you save me? When you must have known what and where I was aiming for?"

The Lord smiled "So you know me then," he replied.

"Yes, we do," Julie told him.

"And we know you took my notebook from our room," Alex replied.

"Aye, I'm sorry about that," Gabriel told him. "Yes, I am after the Gold Mine, but not at the expense of more lives being lost. Like you, I don't need any more money, yes I do know about you selling the painting, is that where you found the first clue?"

"Kind of," Julie replied.

"And you must know how I got my money," Gabriel asked them.

"Yes," Alex replied. "You won it on the lottery."

"Aye I did," Gabriel told him. "My family lost everything searching for Arthur's Cavern, everything, and now that I am close to finding it I don't even need the money."

"When why waste your time searching?" Julie asked.

"I need to prove that it exists," Gabriel replied. "If I prove that it's real, then my family will no longer be a laughing stock, all I want is my family's good name back where it belongs." Gabriel looked down where Alex was sitting on the rocks. "Why don't we work together?" he asked. "It'll be a lot safer with us two on board."

Alex looked up at Julie who nodded back to him "Fair enough," Alex said as he offered his hand to Gabriel. Gabriel pulled him up and once on his feet Alex looked back towards the cave. "Blast it," he cried. "We can't do anything now, the tides going out."

"How high up is the clue?" Joseph asked.

"Too high to reach by hand," Julie replied. "That's why he was trying to swim up to it."

"What about if you stood on yon boy's shoulders?" Gabriel asked.

Julie looked at Alex who looked back to the Lord with a smile on his face "You know," he said. "That might just work."

"Well, come on then, let's do it," Gabriel shouted as he slapped Alex across the back and walked through the knee-deep water towards the cave.

"You'll have to lend me your torch, I've lost mine," Alex told Julie.

Julie pulled Alex back towards her "I'm not sure about this," she told him. "We don't know if we can trust them."

"They saved my life," Alex replied. "They could just have easily let me drown and gone for the clue themselves, we might not know them enough to trust them, but we owe them enough to believe them."

"You're right to be suspicious," Gabriel told them on overhearing their conversation. "Especially about dealing with my family, but believe me, I'm different I'm not a greedy man, just a curious one," he laughed as he slapped Joseph on the back "Curious, aye that's me."

Joseph looked back to Alex and Julie and shrugged his shoulders "He'll grow on you," he laughed as he followed Gabriel in wading through the water.

As they reached the cave, Alex looked up the dripping walls and pointed up to the ledge "It's up there behind that ledge," he cried. "We should be able to reach it," he told them as he looked at the size of Joseph.

Joseph bent down and allowed Alex to step on his shoulders and then with Alex gripping the wall Joseph lifted himself up until he was straight against the wall. "Have you got it," he cried as his shoulders started to buckle. "You're not the lightest of men."

"Almost there," Alex said to himself as he just managed to reach inside the slit behind the ledge. "Bugger," he cried. "It drops down behind the ledge, I can just feel the tip of something metal, I need to go a touch higher."

"Grab hold of something," Gabriel shouted. "I'll lie on the floor and he can use me as a stepping stone." The Lord lay down in the quickly departing salty waters of the Celtic Sea. "Be quick lad," He shouted as he looked up towards Julie. "The water tastes dreadful."

With the extra bit of height, Alex could now look into the slit "Got you, my beauty," he cried as he managed to prise a small metal role out of the slit. "Got it, you can let me down now."

"Thank Christ for that," Joseph cried as Alex finally got off his back.

"What is it?" a dripping wet Gabriel asked.

"Looked like a rolling pin," Joseph replied.

"It's a printer's roller," Julie cried. "I've seen some before, what you do is dip it into some ink and roll it on a piece of paper and it will reveal a message or picture."

"Very clever," Gabriel replied. "The minds of the generation way before us were outstanding."

"Well, we can't do anything here," Alex told them. "Let's get back to our guest house and see what it says, I'll have to get out of these clothes, I'm soaking."

"You're not the only one," Gabriel laughed.

As they made their way up past the chapel, Gabriel told them that they had been following them and that they were all staying in the same pub, he forgot to mention that it was them who had destroyed Alex's car, he thought it best to keep silence about it. After a quick shower, they met up in Alex's room for the big unveiling.

"How does it work?" Joseph asked as they all sat around the table in Alex's room.

"It has ridges all around the cylinder," Julie replied. "I guess we smother it in ink and roll it over the paper by the handles."

"We haven't any ink," Alex told her.

"It doesn't have to be ink," Julie replied. "Any coloured liquid will do, I suppose."

They looked around the room for anything that would do "What about this?" Joseph cried as he grabbed a tomato ketchup bottle.

Julie nodded and grabbed the bottle of him. She ripped the bottom off a box of paper tissues and laid it on the table. "Here goes," she said as she smoothed the sauce around the cylinder and pressed it onto the card and rolled it over. "Can you make out what it says?" Julie asked as she removed the roller.

PONTARFYNACH LIT
BELOW BRIDGE OF THE MYNACH
LAY ON BACK
WHERE OL'E NICK'S WALKED
PASSAGE BE FOUND TO GLORIOUS HILL

"Glorious hill," Gabriel cried. "That must mean the hill where Arthur lays, two more trips and it's ours."

"Nothing's that simple," Alex told him. "Besides we have to decipher the clue yet, Pontarfynach Lit and Bridge of the Mynach."

"Ol'e Nick was obviously the Devil," Julie replied. "But where did he walk?"

"We need the Internet," Joseph told her. "Have you got a laptop here?"

"Over there," Alex told him.

Joseph grabbed the laptop and put it on the table next to the clue. "Right let's see what we can find," he told them as he blew on his hands before keying in Bridge of the Mynach. "This must be it," he cried. "The Devil's Bridge, near Aberystwyth in Wales.

Devil's Bridge, Ceredigion

The main feature of Pontarfynach is the bridge of the same name which spans the Mynach, a tributary of the Rheidol. The bridge is unusual in that three separate bridges are coexistent, each one built upon the previous bridge. The most recently built is an iron bridge (1901), which was built over a stone bridge (1753) which was built when the original bridge (built 1075-1200) was thought to be unstable. The builders of the 1753 bridge used the original bridge to support scaffolding during construction.

The bridge is at a point where the River Mynach drops 300 feet in five steps down a steep and narrow ravine before it meets the River Rheidol. The set of stone steps leading down to the lowest bridge at the waterfall are known as Jacob's ladder.

According to the legend the original bridge was built by the Devil, as it was too difficult for mortals to build. The agreement stipulated that the Devil would build the bridge in return for the soul of the first life to cross the bridge. The

Devil built the bridge but was tricked by an old woman who threw a piece of bread onto the bridge. Her dog crossed the bridge chasing the bread; this becoming the first life to cross it, the Devil disappeared in a rage on being tricked by a mere mortal.

Chapter Five

Devil's Bridge

Devil's Bridge Falls

"Look at the picture of it," Julie cried as a photo of the bridge came up on the screen.

"The clue must be etched into the bottom of the second bridge," Alex told them as he pointed to the picture.

"How the hell do we get down to it?" Joseph asked.

"We could lower somebody down on a rope from the new bridge," Gabriel replied.

"Count me out," Alex cried. "I'm scared of heights; I'm not dangling from a rope over a 300 feet drop."

"We'll cross that bridge, when we get to the bridge if you know what I mean," laughed Gabriel.

"We'll need somewhere to stay," Gabriel told them. "See if there's a hotel nearby it."

"Here's one," Joseph replied. "The Hafod Arms Hotel, quite close to the bridge, shall I book us all in." Within a couple of minutes, Joseph had booked three rooms in the hotel for them and they started to pack straight away so that they could set off first thing in the morning.

They set off in the morning; Alex still didn't fully trust Gabriel so they each took their own car. This time though both cars drove the same way. They started off on the A477 to Milford Haven, where they picked up the A4076 to Haverfordwest, and then they drove for what seemed like hours through the Pembrokeshire National Park along the B4329.

Eventually, they found their way onto the coast road (A487) and stopped for some lunch in a village called Brynhoffnant that lay between Cardigan and Aberaeron.

After lunch, they restarted their journey to Devil's Bridge. The A487 coast road was absolutely packed with traffic and the going was very slow indeed. Every time they managed to pass the slowest moving vehicle in front of them, it was immediately replaced by something even slower, caravans, tractors and even massive 40 feet container lorries. A journey that on paper looked like only a couple of hours drive dragged on and on until, eventually, they reached the city of Aberystwyth and from there it was only a 40-minute drive over the A4120 to the village of Devil's Bridge where they had booked into the Hafod Arms Hotel.

They parked their cars in a car park just before the bridge and walked over to the Hafod Arms Hotel which stood on the next corner about two-minute walk from the bridge. After checking in and refreshing themselves, they all had a walk to the bridge to inspect it to make ready for their attempt at gaining the next clue in the morning. "My God!" cried Joseph as he looked over the bridge and down into the ravine. "That looks a long drop, where're the other bridges?"

"Right under us," Julie replied. "They are all built over one another."

"How do we get to it?" Gabriel asked.

"There are some steps over there," Alex told him. "Maybe they lead down to the original bridge."

They walked over to the path that led down the side of the ravine. They accessed the path via coin-operated turnstiles that lay next to a small ice cream shop on their side and a small souvenir shop on the other. It was packed with tourists on both sides of the pavements and once they paid to go down the steps the pathway down was full of tourists too.

The steep path led by the side of the bridges all the way down to the valley floor affording wonderful views of the cascading falls. It afforded magnificent views of the chasms hewn by the raging torrent from the rock. It also allowed a very close view of the three bridges, but alas no clear way of getting up to the original bridge.

The walls were too steep to climb and even if you could get some footholds in the ageing brickwork one minor slip and you would fall 300 feet into the ravine and to certain death.

They got a tantalising view of the undercarriage of the second bridge but no matter how close in Alex could zoom with his camcorder he couldn't see any etchings or anything else of interest.

After close examinations of the bridges and surroundings, they realised that the only way of getting onto the original bridge was by climbing down a rope from the top bridge. It would be dangerous, very dangerous but there were plenty of rails on the top bridge that should easily support a man's weight.

There was nothing that they could do today so they decided to wait until the next morning. They then made their way back up the steep path and went back to the hotel to get some well-earned rest. After spending the evening having drinks with Gabriel and Joseph, Alex and Julie left them both in the bar while they went up to bed.

While Julie slept something disturbed her and she jumped up "Shh," Alex told her as he put his finger to his lips.

"What are you doing?" she asked as she rubbed the sleep from her eyes. "What time was it?"

"Go back to sleep," he told her.

"Where are you going? You're going to the bridge aren't you?"

Alex nodded "I still don't trust them, they killed my car remember."

"But it's dark out there and you can't go, you're scared of heights remember."

Alex smiled at her. "The reason I'm scared is that I could see how far the drop was, it's dark now, all I'll be able to see is where I shine the torch, you don't have to come, I'll be alright."

But Julie wouldn't let him go by himself, it wasn't that she didn't trust him; it was more like she felt she had to be by his side, just in case something happened. They crept down to the hotel foyer and quietly closed the door as they left the hotel.

They got the rope from the car boot; it was still soaking from the other day when it pulled Alex to safety. "Are you sure about this?" Julie asked as they tied the rope around the rails of the top bridge and around the rails on the other side so that Julie could lower him down. For extra safety, she tied it around her waist so that she could control how much slack Alex got as she lowered him.

Alex nodded as he tied the other end of the rope around his chest and under his shoulders. "Pull on the rope," he told her. "See if it slips." Julie pulled and the rope felt secure enough for Alex to have enough belief that it would hold him safe. Julie gave him a hug and a kiss as he climbed over the rail. "Don't lose the torch," she told him. "It's our last one."

Alex gave out a nervous laugh as he again checked the rope. "Right I'm gonna step off," he cried as he leant out "I can see the fencing of the middle bridge if I can swing in a bit I should be able to get a foothold and from there I should be okay," he gave her a nod, and she released some slack.

He took a deep breath and let go of the rail, he didn't feel safe enough to step off, and instead, he knelt down and gripped the bottom of the rail and slowly slid down. With his hands holding onto the bottom rail, he fumbled with his feet until he felt them strike something hard.

"Right I've got my bearings, you can release some more slack," he cried as he let go of the rail. She slowly lowered him down and he soon passed the walkway of the middle bridge. "Shit," he cried as he felt the damp rope unknotting itself from around his waist.

Up on top of the bridge, Julie was peering over into a chasm of darkness and then she heard some shouting. She looked over to the road and saw two men shouting and screaming and running towards her. The shock made her forget what she was doing and the rope slipped from around her waist.

Down below Alex was screaming to her to pull him up as the sudden release of tension on the rope dropped him well below the original bridge and caused the damp rope to slip away from his chest and his fingers could not get enough grip on the rope. He was losing the rope; he knew that soon the rope would be out of his hands so he made a conscious decision to reach for the hole in the original bridge where the water was cascading from.

He just managed to grip the wet rock as he lost the rope. He was holding on for dear life, struggling desperately to get a foothold. But the cascading water was too strong for every time he looked up to try to see another place to grab a hold of the icy cold water kept splashing into his face, filling his mouth with the dirty waters of the River Mynach.

As he spat out another mouthful of water, he saw the green branches of an overgrown tree sticking out from over the edge of the bridge. His only chance of salvation was to try to reach out and grab the closest branch. It was in reachable range, the only problem was he would have to let go of the waterfall ridge to reach it. He again cleared his mouth of dirty water, and with every ounce of his remaining strength, he leapt for the branch.

He cried out with relief as he got a good grip on the branch and managed to gain a foothold in the decaying brickwork. He gripped the branch further up and began to walk up the face of the bridge. He cheered as his feet stood on the edge of the bridge and he could finally let go of the tree. He stood on the edge and looked up to shout to Julie that he was alright, but to his horror the decaying brickwork on the edge gave way and he fell backwards over the edge and into the ravine.

"Alex!" Julie screamed as she heard Alex's deathly cry.

"Julie, Julie, wake up you've been dreaming," Alex cried as Julie's scream woke him up. Julie shot up from her pillow with sweat pouring down her forehead and grabbed him and pulled him close to her. "What is it?" he asked as he stroked her damp blonde hair. "What did you see?"

It took her a few seconds to catch her breath, and before she spoke, she hugged him again and kissed him. "I had a nightmare," she told him as she wiped the sweat from her brow.

"What about?" he asked.

"You," she replied. "It was like the one I had last year about Pete, you know when I dreamt about the car crash the night he died."

"What happened in your dream? What happened to me?" he asked. "Hey, calm down," he told her tenderly as she started to cry. "It was only a dream, I'm fine."

"It was so real," she sobbed. "I saw you fall, you were climbing down the Devil's Bridge. You fell."

"That's stupid," he replied as he wiped away her tears. "You know how scared of heights I am. Do you honestly think I'll climb down to a bridge 300 feet high?"

"You said that you'd be alright because it was dark, if you couldn't see how high it was you'd be alright, but you fell, I heard you yell."

"Come here, you daft sod," he replied as he pulled out a paper tissue for her to blow her nose. "This one won't come true, there's no way I'm climbing down those bridges, no way at all."

"Promise me," she pleaded. "Promise me, that no matter what, you will never climb down the bridge, promise me."

He held her head against his bare chest and stroked her naked back "I promise you," he whispered to her. "I will never climb that bridge."

He lifted her face up to his and kissed her tenderly on her lips. "The only thing I care about is you and I'm not going to risk losing you, you're all I have." He kissed her again and then told her that she must try to get some sleep as they had a busy day ahead of them. She cuddled into him and held him tight as she dozed off.

The next morning before breakfast, they met up with Gabriel and Joseph in the car park, they had decided that their only chance of getting onto the bottom bridge unnoticed was by going to it before the tourists arrive and the two shops were closed. It was a cold and breezy spring morning with a hint of a storm coming.

"I think we should make hay while the sun shines," Gabriel told them. "By the look of the clouds over there, we won't have much more sun left before the storm hits us."

While Julie and Alex paid to go down the path to the left of the bridge, Gabriel and Joseph walked down the right-hand side. Both parties zoomed their cameras into the underneath of the middle bridge but both without success for nothing could be seen. Alex shouted over the ravine to tell them that they'll meet up with them both at the top. As they eventually reached the top bridge, they saw the steam of a locomotive, which passed them by on its journey into the Devil's Bridge railway station. "That has to be a sign," Alex told Julie. "Seeing a steam train in this day and age, at this particular time, it's uncanny."

"You could be right," Julie replied. "Hey, look it's Laurel and Hardy," she laughed as Gabriel and Joseph appeared on the other end of the bridge.

Gabriel whispered something to Joseph, who nodded back to him. On meeting up with Alex and Julie, they decided again that their only hope of retrieving the clue was by lowering someone down by rope. Alex ran back to the car to get the still damp rope out of the boot and carried it back. "Who's going down?" he asked as he got back to the bridge.

Gabriel and Joseph looked at one another and both replied in tandem "You."

Alex laughed out loud "Yeah, sure I am," he told them.

"We're not joking pal," Joseph replied. "You are going down there."

"The hell I am," Alex shouted. "And you can't make me."

"Wanna bet," cried Joseph as he grabbed Julie's neck in his arm.

"Let her go," Alex screamed as he moved towards Joseph.

"Hang on there, son," Gabriel shouted as he pulled out a small pistol and pointed it into Alex's face. He nodded to the rope on the floor "We are not messing about, now either you tie that rope around you and agree to slide down it or…"

"Or what?" Alex cried as he interrupted the Lord. "You're gonna shoot me, you haven't got it in you."

"Don't test me, son," Gabriel shouted back. "This is your last warning now pick up the rope and go and get us the last clue."

"Don't do it, Alex," Julie cried. "He won't shoot you; he needs you to get the clue, for he and mate here haven't the bottle to go themselves."

"Hey, you're right there lass, we do need him," Gabriel shouted. "But we don't need you," he pulled the gun away from Alex's face and trained it towards Julie's stomach "Do you want kids?" he growled. "Then for the last time, get the rope around your waist now."

Alex looked towards his wife, who was still held in a headlock by Joseph. She shook her head "My dream, remember my dream, if you go down there you fall, remember Pete, I dreamt his death remember."

"I've no choice," Alex replied as he picked up the rope. "They're a murderous family are the Farthingay's, always were and always will be, you don't want the money for your family, you want it for yourself, beware the greedy man, that's what Concerve said, he knew that your family would never give up the search, well I hope you bloody choke on it."

"Sorry about this love," Joseph whispered into Julie's ear just before he let her go.

"Don't think about running or screaming," Gabriel told her as he motioned her to join Alex by the rail. "You do anything to annoy me and we leave him down there."

"I'll be good," she replied. "Just don't let go of the rope, he's terrified of heights."

"Then you are shit out of luck," Joseph laughed as he tightened the damp rope around Alex. "Is it secure?"

Alex nodded "Good," replied Gabriel. "We wouldn't want you to fall down this mighty drop would we, well not before you get the clue."

Joseph looked over the edge of the rail and laughed "300 feet, but at least you'll have a soft landing in the river below."

"Hey," said the Lord. "But only if you miss the rocks on both sides, I say this lad, if you fall then keep your body straight and you just may make it."

"Very funny," Alex cried as he climbed over the rail. "Just make sure that the damn rope doesn't slip."

"Let me go instead," Julie pleaded. "Look at him he's terrified, I'm a much better climber, I've got a better grip."

"Too late lass, he's going," Gabriel told her as he pointed the gun back to her head.

"Alright, alright," Alex cried as he let go of the rail. "If I keep my eyes on you bastards then I'll be okay, lower me, but lower me slowly."

"As you wish," Gabriel replied as he and Joseph let some slack into the rope.

"Don't look down," Alex told himself. "Keep focusing up, don't look down."

Julie stood overlooking the side of the bridge with her thumb in her mouth "Alex," she shouted down to him. "Keep your eyes set on me and forget about where you are, look at me and imagine it's me who's going up."

"He's quite safe," Joseph told her. "I won't drop him, I promise."

"Aye, he's quite strong is our Joseph and I'm no weakling, he'll be alright," Gabriel shouted to her.

"Move me over a bit," Alex cried as he was being lowered onto the overhanging tree. "To the left," he shouted.

"That'll do," Julie shouted to Gabriel. "He's got his feet on the ledge."

"Is he in?" Gabriel shouted.

"I need a bit more slack," Alex shouted as he tried to duck under the arch of the middle bridge. "Right," he shouted up to them. "I'm in."

"Is he in yet?" Joseph asked.

Julie nodded so both men unwrapped the rope from their arms and secured it to the back rail. Down below them Alex had released himself from the rope and lay down on his back and shuffled under the bridge. He was struggling to find room to move as the archway where he lay was smothered with centuries of wild growth.

"Now where would he leave the clue?" Alex asked himself as he shone the torch around the centre of the arch. He couldn't see anything so he shuffled further under. His path was hard going and he had to keep snapping branches and weeds out from under his way.

"What did the clue say?" he asked himself again. "Lay on your back, where Ol'e Nick walked, well I'm on my bloody back, where the bloody heck was the clue, there has to be another Rocket Emblem, but where?"

He thought to put himself in Conserve's shoes, where would he put the clue if it was he who had left it. He knew that it wouldn't be at the start of the archway because there wasn't enough room for a man to sit up and etch anything into the brickwork. It had to be in the middle, but where. He started to scrape at the moss-covered bricks in the centre to see if he could unearth anything.

"He's taking his time isn't he?" cried Gabriel. "Has he fallen asleep?"

"Give him a chance," Julie barked back at him. "The clue was left over 150 years ago; he'd have to clear over a century of overgrowth from down there."

"I only said he was taking his time," Gabriel replied. "You don't have to talk to me as I'm shit."

"Well, pardon me," Julie snapped back. "If you're not happy, then why don't you slide down there and help him."

"I don't know what you're grinning at," Gabriel shouted to a smiling Joseph. "If he's not back up within the next 10 minutes you are going down there."

"I told you I would have in the first place," Joseph replied. "It was you who wanted him to go down."

"Well, how could I know he was scared of heights, I'm no mind reader," Gabriel told him.

"You should have asked," Julie cried. "For all we know, he could be catatonic down there." Just then Julie's mobile phone started to buzz. "It's Alex," she told them.

"Well, has he found it?" Gabriel asked as Julie put her phone away.

"Yes," she replied. "He's just unearthed the emblem and he's sure the clue must be nearby."

Down below Alex was still scraping the moss away; he had found the emblem so he knew that he was quite close to the clue. Just then he found some etching to the right of the emblem, five lines above what looked like a small map etched into the brickwork. He held the torch in his mouth while he wrote it down in his notebook.

FOLLOW WHAT FALLS

FIVE TIMES

TO POLE

ON ARTHURS

MOUNT

Once he had written down the clue, Alex phoned Julie's mobile again to let her know that he was ready to come back up. She phoned him back to tell them that once the rope was secure they'll waggle it about so he knew that it was safe. He tied the rope back around him and pulled on it to make sure that it was secure.

Then he saw the slack of the rope waggle and slowly being pulled up. Once all the slack had been tensioned, he took a deep breath and stood on the edge of the Devil's Bridge and looked up. He couldn't see to the top of the newest bridge because the new bridge shot out over the two old bridges.

He took another deep breath as he felt the rope being pulled. He gripped the rope and held on for dear life as he got slowly pulled up past the middle bridge. "Almost there," he heard Julie shout as he looked up and saw her deep blue eyes looking down at him.

As he reached the safety of the top bridge, he gripped hold of the rail and pulled himself up.

"Oh no, you don't," Gabriel told him as he stopped him from climbing over. "I didn't say that you could come over did I."

"Stop fooling about," Julie shouted. "He's done all that you asked."

The lord smiled and again pointed his gun towards her "Do you see the clue, in my hands yet," he told her.

"Give him a chance," she cried. "He isn't up yet."

"Give us the clue," Gabriel cried to Alex. "The clue or no wifey."

"It's in my notebook," Alex shouted as he reached into his back pocket. "Shit," he cried as his mobile phone fell from his jacket breast pocket as he bent down to retrieve the notebook.

"You can always get a new phone," Gabriel told him. "Now hand the book to Joseph," Gabriel told him.

"Don't, Alex," Julie cried. "If you give it to him, he'll cut you lose."

The lord laughed out loud "Don't be so stupid, girl, I'm no killer."

"So you'll let him up then?" she asked him.

"I never said that," Gabriel replied. "But if he hands me the notebook, I promise you that I won't harm either of you."

"We've no choice love," Alex told her as he handed Joseph the notebook. "It's the last page that it's written on," he told Gabriel as Joseph opened it.

"Aye, you've done all I asked," Gabriel replied. "But you must know that I can't let you go."

"But you promised," Julie cried.

"I promised not to harm you, I never said anything about letting you go, he's going back down, but don't worry love so are you."

"What!" she cried. "You can't be serious."

Gabriel smiled as he told her that indeed he was serious "The only way I can be sure of finding the cavern before you is to make sure that I get a decent head start, so I'm not going to kill you, but I am going to leave you stranded down there, but don't worry once we are away from here we'll leave a signal so people will come for you."

Julie growled towards the Lord as they again lowered Alex down to the Devil's Bridge. Once Alex was safely on the bridge, they dragged the rope back up and then lowered Julie down. But just as they were lowering her, she felt herself being dragged back up. A confused Julie looked up at the grinning Lord.

"What now?" she shouted to them.

"You think I'm stupid don't you?" Gabriel told her. "Well, I'm not that stupid, your phone please, and don't bother stretching to give it to me, just tip it out your little hand and let it fall, that'll be good enough."

Julie shook her head as she dropped her phone into the gaping chasm below her.

"Right," Gabriel shouted. "Tatty bye," he told her as they lowered her down. Alex grabbed hold of her as she dangled by the bottom bridge and pulled into the safety of the bridge. "I'm sorry," she cried as he hugged her. "There was nowt I could I do."

"It's okay, my love," he replied as he kissed her.

"There's not much room," she told him as she sat down on the ledge.

"Do you mind not sitting there," he nervously asked her.

"I'm not gonna fall," she told him but on seeing the look in his eyes she lifted up her legs and shuffled over to where he sat. "Where did you find the clue?" she asked him.

"Over there," he told her. "If you lie on your back and shuffle under you'll see it."

"Do you see it?" he asked her as she shuffled under. "Do you see the Rocket Emblem?"

"Yes," she replied. "Do you know what it means?"

"Yes, but we'll have to be quick if we want to reach it before they get back."

"What do you mean before they get back?" she asked him.

"Well, I told you that I still didn't trust them, didn't I?"

"Yes."

"So I've given them a false clue."

"You didn't."

"I did," he laughed. "I've sent them to Conway."

"Conway?" she asked.

"Yes, Conway, there's a railway bridge between Llandudno Junction and Conway, it was finished in 1848, I noticed it when I was looking Stephenson up on the web, I wrote down the details of it in my notebook just in case any clues took us there, so while I was down here I made up a clue from the information that I had. The real clue is written on the back of my original info and is under that rock there, I thought I'd best be safe."

"You're brilliant you know that," she cried as she scrambled back to him and kissed him. Above them, Gabriel was explaining the clue to Joseph.

BRIDGE BUILT 1848
AFON CONWAY
15 PIER
UNDER CARRIAGE
LAY ROCKET TO CAVERN OF GOLD

"We need the internet straight away," Joseph told him. "See what it means?"

"Don't have to lad," Gabriel told him. "I think I know."

"Know what?"

"In my ancestor's journals, he mentioned all the places where Stephenson had travelled in Wales. And did you know that Stephenson built a bridge between Llandudno and Conway? And I'm sure that a river separates the two towns and Afon means River in Welsh."

"I must admit, you're a clever bugger at times, sir."

"Not clever lad, just a good memory, so let's get a move on, go back to the hotel, pack our bags and let's make history."

"I thought you were gonna leave a signal to help them two out?" Joseph asked him as they were walking towards their car.

"So I was," Gabriel replied. "Have you got your lighter there?"

"Yes, what do you want it for?"

"I always did like a good fire," Gabriel replied as he took the lighter from him. "This time the car will burn," he told him as he picked up an old rag of the floor. He unscrewed the petrol cap off Alex's Red Corsa and dipped it in the rag and set fire to it. "Right let's be off before it explodes." They ran to their car and drove off. Within minutes, the car was alight and exploded into flames.

"What was that?" Julie cried on hearing the explosion.

"I hope it's not what I think it is," Alex replied. "I've got a feeling he's killed my car again the bastard."

"Forget about it," Julie laughed. "We can always get another car, what we need to do is to get off this bridge."

"First thing I do," Alex told her. "The very first thing that I do when I next meet that bastard is kill his God damn car."

Julie smiled at her grumbling husband "Once we're off here, you can do as you please, but first, we need a plan. Can't we drop down to that ledge?"

Alex slowly leant over and looked down "Bugger me, I'm going dizzy," he cried.

"My God, they breed them hard in Basingstoke don't they," Julie replied.

"I can't help it," he told her. "It's a medical condition, it's not a joke."

"Okay, then I'll see if I can drop down, don't worry I've got perfect grip and balance, us northerners don't crack so easy," she replied as she gripped hold of the ledge and slowly lowered herself down.

Alex composed himself and shuffled over to the ledge "You've got no chance," he told her as he found the courage to look down. "You're still not even halfway to the ledge and it's only a small ledge, if you drop you may slip over, it's not worth the risk." He helped her back up and they sat back down.

"You know," she cried as she looked up. "I think it'll be easier going up, if you look there where the wall of the second bridge passes this one I should be able to use both walls and climb up it, I should get to the middle bridge dead easy."

Alex looked up "It looks possible, but I don't think that I'll be able to climb it, I'm not soft but you don't understand the fear that drives through me every time I look up or down this blasted bridge."

"It's okay, my love," she told him. "I understand, I will go up and once I'm up I'll get help so as you are not stranded anymore."

She kissed him on the lips before starting her journey up the ancient walls. She actually found it quite easy-going, the cracks in the walls were perfect for her small nimble fingers, she got finger holds after finger holds and found plenty of footholds to support her. Within five minutes, she was on top of the middle bridge.

Once on top of that bridge, she worked her way along the edge of it by carefully leaning into the old railings on it. When she got to the end of the bridge there was an overgrown tree sticking out which looked like it would support her weight. She grabbed hold of the thickest branch that she could see and gently pulled herself onto the tree and from there she casually dropped onto the footpath by the ravine's side.

"That was simple," she thought to herself as she raced down the path that over looked the bridges. "I made it," she shouted as she waved to her husband. Alex smiled with relief and waved back to her. "I'll make my way to the top and get help," she told him. She blew him a kiss and raced up the steep path.

When she finally got to the top bridge she cried with relief on seeing that Gabriel had left the rope still tied to the bridge. "Thank God," she shouted as she pulled on the rope to check it was still secured to the back rail. She then shouted down to Alex and lowered the rope to him.

On grabbing the rope, he tied it around his waist and gripped the rope above him. He knew that Julie wouldn't have the strength to pull him up so he would have to walk up the side of the bridges. He took a deep breath and jumped up the rope and shimmied up it until his feet touched the walls of the second bridge.

The rope was still damp from the time by the seashore but Alex was gripping it with all his might and he was actually making good headway. As he reached the top of the middle bridge, he grabbed the old railings and took a breather.

But just as he was set back on his way the old decaying railing gave way and Alex plunged back down. Luckily the rope held firm leaving him dangling just above the Devil's Bridge "I'm okay," he yelled. "Just a slight miss-hap, give me a minute and I'll start again."

Julie looked on helpless as her husband was swinging in the bustling wind above a 300 feet drop. "Hoy you," she heard a voice cry. She looked up to see two men shouting and screaming and running towards her. The shock of seeing them brought back memories of her dream and the rope slipped from her grasp and started to unravel from her waist.

"My God," she cried. "This is my dream, Alex!" she shouted as the rope left the rail.

Alex cried out as the sudden slack to the rope dropped him below the Devil's bridge, but luckily the rope got tangled around the back rail of the top bridge and Alex was left dangling over the 300 feet drop.

As he twirled around on the rope, he cried out to Julie to find out what had happened but as the rope dropped him further into the ravine he started to panic. He could feel the brisk wind as it bellowed across his face and as it spun him around he could see the jagged edges of the rocky ravine around him. He cried out for Julie to pull him up, again and again, he cried but the rope kept pushing him further down.

Up on top of the bridge the two men had reached Julie, to her relief they hadn't been shouting at her, they were chasing their dog, a black and white collie that had run too far in front of them. They noticed immediately that Julie was in distress.

"Grab the rope," she screamed as it slipped from the back rail.

"What?" the first man cried.

"The rope," Julie screamed. "My husband's down there grab the rope."

"Mate, give me a hand," the man cried to his friend. "I can't hold it, it's slipping, the ropes too wet."

His mate grabbed hold of the rope with him and together they managed to secure it once again around the back rail. Julie shouted down to Alex that it was alright now, but he couldn't hear her. The shock of dropping into the gaping chasm had made him faint and his limp body was swirling around in the howling wind.

With Julie also helping, they managed to pull Alex up to safety. Once he was up against the top rail, they secured the rope and both men dragged him over just as he was coming around. On finally placing his feet onto solid ground, Alex hugged Julie, and they both thanked the two men who then carried on with chasing their dog.

"The bastard," Alex cried as he saw the thick black smoke coming from where his car was parked. They both ran over the bridge and to the lay-by where the Red Corsa was smouldering away. "I swear," Alex shouted. "The next time we meet I'm gonna kill that bloody car of theirs, you'll see, I will I'll bloody kill it."

"Calm down lover," Julie told him as she placed her arm over his shoulder. "We'll get them back for sure, but the best way to make him suffer was to find the treasure before he did."

Alex took a last look at his car and then they walked the two miles back to the Hafod Arms Hotel. Once in the room, they picked up their A to Z of Wales to see where the map on the clue led them to.

"The River Mynach drops five steps 300 feet to where it meets the River Rheidol," Julie told him as she read the info of the Devil's Bridge. "So what falls five times was the River, so follow the river to Arthur's Mount."

"There's a mountain right at the base of the River Rheidol where it enters the sea," Alex told her as he followed the river by the map. "Pen Dinas it's called."

"Pen Dinas," Julie asked him as she keyed it into her laptop. "Here it is, Pen Dinas, An Iron Age Hill Fort, Hey look at this what lies on top of it."

"What is it?" Alex asked.

"It's Arthur's Mount okay," She told him, just isn't King Arthur, but it's the next best thing."

"Who is it then?"

"Arthur Wellesley, Duke of Wellington, apparently there's a cannon ball-shaped monument on there."

"The clue must be on the monument," Alex told her. "How far is it?"

"Are we gonna get another car or shall we be daring and do it Conserve's way."

"You mean walk?"

"Well, we could," Julie told him. "It could take us ages to buy a new car, I suppose we could take a taxi, but Gabriel could already be on his way back, the less people who know where we're going the better if we follow the river we can't go wrong."

"I guess it's the safest option, hang on a sec, doesn't that mean that we have to go down the steep path by the side of the bridge."

"Don't be a babbie," she laughed. "Grab your coat; it's gonna be cold down there."

"The things I do for love," Alex muttered as he followed her out of the hotel room.

On reaching the bridge, they paid at the coin-operated turnstile and carefully made their way down the steep path and descended to the valley below. When they reached the floor of the valley they started their way along the path that ran beside the River Rheidol.

Below the waterfalls, the river passed the abandoned workings of the Cwn Rheidol Lead Mine and after passing that they made their way through the heavily afforested area. It was a long journey that they were making, especially by foot but the scenery was spectacular enough to compensate for the arduous journey. After two hours of hard walk, they reached the village of Capel Seton where they stopped by a local public house and had a bit of refreshment.

Somewhere along the A470 quite close to Betws-y-Coed Gabriel was driving angrily back to Devil's Bridge. He had wasted nearly two hours driving to Conway only to find it was a wasted journey and now he had another couple of hours before he got back to Devil's Bridge. He was hoping against all odds that Alex and Julie were still trapped on the bridge but he sensed that they were free and had already reached the final clue.

After their refreshments, Alex and Julie continued with their journey. The remainder of the meandering course of the river was through an ever-widening valley where eventually the river discharged itself into the sea through Aberystwyth Harbour. Once they reached there, Alex and Julie had another hour's walk to the top of Arthur's or as it's called Pen Dinas.

Pen Dinas

Just on the southern edge of Aberystwyth lies this 114-metre high hill. Once home to an Iron Age fort, the hill is also recognisable for the distinctive monument perched on top. As far as the history of the site goes, it is known that a fort was built at the summit around 400 BC.

More recently, Pen Dinas saw the addition of a chimney-like monument on top. This well-known local monument was built in 1852 in memory of the Duke of Wellington, Victor of Waterloo was paid for by public subscription, it was planned to be even grander and topped with a statue of a man on horseback, but money ran out, leaving it how it is today.

A climb up to the top of the hill on a pleasant day is very rewarding as you can see for miles inland along both the Ystwyth and Rheidol River valleys, as well as a way out to sea. It's also a brilliant spot to picnic if you avoid windy days.

Eventually, Gabriel finally reached the Devil's Bridge and on seeing the rope tossed by the side of it instantly realised that they had got free. At first, he ordered Joseph to climb down the rope and find the clue, but then Joseph told him that it would be easier to go back to the Hafod Arms Hotel and try to trace them online.

For he had remembered that he had put a bug into Alex's laptop and if they had logged on to try to fathom the clue out, then they would instantly know where they were heading. Once back at the hotel, Gabriel watched as Joseph tried to log into Alex's home page on his computer so that he could trace the sites that Alex had been clicked onto.

"Can't get in," Joseph told him. "Computer must be switched off."

"What? Now then," Gabriel asked.

"I suppose we can have a look in their room, if they're not in, they may have left their laptop there."

"Can you get in?" Gabriel asked.

"Piece of piss, in this place, the doors aren't that strong and the locks are even weaker," Joseph told him.

While Gabriel kept watching Joseph quietly placed a plastic card into the door frame between the lock and the casing and gently nudge the door open "Piece of piss, like I told you," Joseph told him as he held the door open for the Lord to enter Alex's room.

"We're in luck," Joseph told him as he spotted the laptop on the table. "Give me a minute and we'll see if they have been back in the last few hours."

"If they've been back, they haven't gone far," Gabriel said as he noticed the clothes were still in the wardrobe.

"Here it is," Joseph told the Lord. "Pen Dinas, that's where they are heading."

"What is it and where is it?" Gabriel asked.

"One minute," Joseph told him as he keyed it into his laptop. "Pen Dinas, right I've got it, bloody hell it's not far from here, look; it's that hill by the coast."

"That's it," Gabriel told him. "That has to be where Arthur's buried."

Chapter Six

Pendinas

Wellington Monument

The only man-made structure on the top of Pen Dinas that they could see when they reached the top was a massive chimney-like monument. It was tall very tall but they couldn't tell how high up it went from where they were standing. The bottom pediment was about 5 feet high and the chimney shot up from that, near the top it had a rim that stuck out that ran around the monument and about 10 feet from there was another rim that seemed to be the top of the structure.

"That must be the pole in the clue," Julie said as she looked up at the tall tower.

"It's the only thing up here," Alex replied. "So the clue must be on it somewhere."

"Here," she cried as she found a plaque on the monument. "In memory of the Duke of Wellington, Victor of Waterloo 1852"

"Well, the date tallies up to Conserve's journal," Alex told her. "So the clue must be on it, but where?"

They searched along the lower pediment; there was loads of graffiti etched into it but it seemed to be from different eras and nothing that was written made any sense to them. If only they could find the Rocket Emblem then they would know what part the clue was on. Julie pulled out the camcorder from her bag and slowly walked around the monument while zooming in to try to find the clue.

Meanwhile, Gabriel and Joseph were on their way to Aberystwyth in their car; they had just passed a signpost showing them the way to Pen Dinas. They managed to drive halfway up but then ran out of the road. On leaving their car, they made their way up the muddy path. "Are you sure that we're going the right way?" Joseph asked as the path they were taking started to go back downhill towards the deserted beach ahead of them.

"Where else can we go?" Gabriel told him.

"We could make our way up there," Joseph replied as he pointed up the grassy hillside.

Gabriel shook his head and grumbled under his breath as he slowly followed Joseph up the grassy slope. As they reached about halfway up the grass and weeds turned into nettles and prickles. After being stung for about the 20th time, they ran out of path and the only way forward was through a 3 feet field of more nettles and prickles. They looked around, and even though they were close to the top and had a good view of the monument, there was no way of reaching it this way so both agreed that the only way was down and to find another path.

It took them another half hour or so to make their way back down to the path, getting stung a lot more times on their way. At the bottom, they continued along the path until they passed two men who were cutting the grass. On asking them if there was a way to the top, they were told to go back the way they came and the path was at the top of the road.

They couldn't be bothered to walk back up the road so they took their car and left it by the stile that led to the path. Joseph told him that he was blocking the path leaving it there but Gabriel just muttered something about there being no traffic coming this way.

"I've found it," cried Julie as she zoomed into the rim around the top of the monument. "I've found the Rocket Emblem."

"Where?" Alex asked as she passed him the camcorder. She pointed to the rim and Alex zoomed into it. "I can see the Emblem," he told her. "But no clue, it must be along the top of the rim."

"How the hell can we reach it?" Julie asked. "We can't actually drag a ladder all the way up here, the wind up here would just blow it over, plus we would be seen from the town."

"There has to be a way," Alex told her as he walked around the perimeter of the monument.

"Shit," Julie cried. "It's them."

"Who's them?" Alex asked.

"Gabriel and the goon," she told him as she pointed down the hill to them.

"Have they seen us?"

"I don't think so."

"Well, let's go before they arrive, we can sneak down by those trees, if we can't reach the clue neither can they, we'll come back later once we have figured out how to get up there."

They just managed to get out of view behind the trees before Joseph reached the top.

"Come on old man," Joseph laughed. "They're not here yet."

"Or they had already been," Gabriel replied as he reached the top. "Bloody mud, my shoes are ruined, do you know how much these buggers cost?"

"Forget about the shoes," Joseph told him. "And try to figure out where the bloody entrance to the cavern is."

"Did you hear that?" Julie whispered. "They think the cavern is under the monument, are they thick or what?" Alex held his finger to his lips and beckoned her to follow him down. Julie looked back up to see the Lord stood with his hands on his hips while Joseph looked around the monument.

"What are you smiling for?" Julie asked as they reached the road.

"That's why I'm smiling," he replied as he pointed to Gabriel's gleaming silver E-type Jaguar. "I'll teach the bastard to kill my cars."

"Oh Alex, you can't," She told him as he picked up a large stone from the grassy verge.

"They killed my cars," he replied.

"But if you do out, they'll know it's us, they ain't that stupid."

"Sod it," he cried as he whacked the brick against the driver's window.

On smashing the window, they were shocked that no alarm went off "See what I mean," Alex told her. "No brains whatsoever, owning a beautiful car like this and not even installing an alarm, they deserved to have it stolen."

"We're not gonna steal it are we?" she asked him as he got into the driver's seat.

"No," he replied. "I'm just taking off the handbrake and getting the steering sorted so as it goes over the hill and down by the sea. Have you still got your notebook in there?"

"Yeah, why?"

"I'm gonna leave them a note pinned over the gear stick, write this down."

Sorry about your beautiful car, but I still owe you one.

We have the next clue; this wasn't the last one,

This isn't Arthur's Mount, check your map,

there's no way that they would have been checking this hill out for a railway to

Porthmadog. The town has its own port.

Once we have found the cavern, we'll let you know

Bye for now

"Hopefully, that'll get them away from here so that we can retrieve the next clue in peace," he told her as he placed the note carefully onto the gear stick. "Hand brake off, now push."

As the car gathered speed, it caught Joseph's attention "Sir," he cried.

"What?" Gabriel asked.

But Joseph couldn't reply he just pointed down the hill. "Holy shit!" Gabriel cried as he saw his car leave the road and fly over the grassy verge and down the side of the hill. "Damn it," he cried as he ran down the hill.

As he ran, he lost his footing on the muddy path and slid down on his backside through the mud. "Are you alright, sir?" Joseph asked as he helped the Lord up. Gabriel didn't reply he shoved Joseph away and carried on running to the end of the path and looked down to see his beloved silver Jag lying in the middle of an old shed that it had demolished on its journey.

"Did you leave the handbrake off?" Joseph asked as they made their way down to the broken car.

"Think I'm stupid lad," Gabriel shouted. "This was no accident; it was the lad and the girl."

"How do you know?"

"I just do, it's their way to tell me they're here, watching, laughing, and sniggering at us," Gabriel couldn't finish his sentence for he again slipped, this time on the damp grass and he slipped down into the rubble that once was his car.

Again Joseph helped him up and as the Lord stood looking at his car with his hands on his hips Joseph looked inside and found the note, still stuck over the gear stick.

"You were right, sir," he told the Lord as he handed him the note.

"Damn Bastards," Gabriel shouted as he read the note. "I know you're here, you bastard," he cried as he looked around the surrounding hill. "I'll find you; I swear I'll bloody find you."

About a hundred yards away Alex was giggling to himself as he peered from the safety of the surrounding bushes. "Are you happy now?" Julie asked him. "Can we get back to work now or have you got another childish prank to play."

"Happy as Larry," Alex told her as he jumped up and clapped his hands. "Let's get a taxi back to the guesthouse and plan our next move.

As they both slipped quietly away from the hill, Gabriel climbed into the wreckage of the car and pulled out his map. "They're right you know," he told Joseph. "This isn't the hill, it's nowhere near, I'm a fool, you're following a fool do you know that?"

"You're no fool, sir," Joseph told him as he threw an arm over Gabriel's shoulder. "You just got carried away that's all, at least my laptop's still working so we still can trace their next moves."

"Aye, but only if they haven't trigged how we have been trailing them they're smarter than I thought."

"They may be smart but I'm smarter," Joseph told him. "I will find them sir; believe me, I'll find them. Where are you going?" he asked as Gabriel started to walk back up the hill."

"If there's a clue up there, then by God I'll find it," Gabriel shouted back. "You salvage what you can from that while I go up and have another look."

On salvaging what he could, Joseph then joined the Lord back at the monument.

"Have you found anything?" he asked.

"Nothing," Gabriel replied. "Nothing, that makes any sense, there's loads of etching on it but I can't understand it, in fact, I don't think any of it is what we are looking for, the clue as to be somewhere else, but where?"

"Don't worry, sir," Joseph told him. "As soon as they go online to figure out the clue, I'll get them, I'll trace them to the ends of the earth to make you feel better."

"Aye, I know you would," Gabriel replied as he threw his arm around him. "Hopefully, it won't be as far as that, come on lad we have to find us somewhere to stay and then we'll need us a new car, in fact, they're gonna need a car as well so if we're lucky we'll find them at the nearest garage.

Back at the Hafod Arms Alex and Julie were sat in the bar enjoying a cool drink while they went over the camcorder footage from Pen Dinas. They knew that there was no way of reaching the top of the monument from the floor, it was too high to climb and there weren't any footholds or finger holes to safely climb up it anyway.

"What we need," Alex told her. "Was Somehow finding a way to photograph the top, you know like satellite maybe."

"Or," Julie replied as she jumped up from her seat and ran over to the doorway.

"What is it?" Alex asked as she came back with a brochure in her hands.

"Helicopter rides," she replied. "I noticed the brochure when we booked in, Whizzard Helicopters."

"Whizzard."

"Yes, Whizzard as in Merlin, Arthur and the Round Table."

"Another coincidence," Alex told her. "It's like we were meant to use this firm, where are they from?"

Whizzard Helicopters is a flight training school and charter business. Providing people with the opportunity to view the spectacular Welsh Scenery from the air. It is based near Welshpool, North Wales

"Not far from here then," Alex told her as he pointed to Welshpool on the map.

"All we need is to get some transport, ride over to Welshpool and book a trip," Julie replied. "I'll phone them up and book us a ride for tomorrow."

They couldn't book for the next day but they did book for the following Saturday, which gave them time to buy yet another car, a black 2007 Vauxhall Corsa, a lot newer than their previous red one. They also bought a new mobile phone each as well to replace the ones they lost on the Devil's Bridge.

Surprisingly there was no sign of his Lordship and Joseph in the last few days, surely, they wouldn't have given up that easily? Alex thought that at least they would have seen them around the hotel but the less they saw of them the better.

The Lord and Joseph hadn't totally given up but they had no lead to follow. They were in fact stopping at another hotel right in the centre of Aberystwyth. Where they were waiting until something popped up on Julie's laptop. From where they were staying they had a good view of the monument from their hotel window, just in case Alex had lied in his note and if indeed he had then they would know as soon as he showed himself on top of Pen Dinas.

Once they arrived at Whizzard Helicopters in Welshpool, Alex's fear of heights hit him again, and he couldn't go up with Julie. It was only a minor hiccup for Julie quite enjoyed the ride; she had taken her camcorder with her so as to get a good photo of the top of the monument. As they arrived over the hill, the buzzing of the helicopter above the hotel drew Joseph to his hotel window.

"What is it?" Gabriel asked as Joseph shouted him over to the window."

"Could be nothing," he replied. "But there is a helicopter hovering over the monument."

Gabriel ran to the window "Where're the binoculars?" he shouted as he saw the copter almost on top of the monument.

Joseph passed him the binoculars "What can you see? Is it them?"

"I'm not sure," Gabriel told him. "There's somebody in the back with a camera pointed at the top of the chimney, hang on a tick I can just make out the colour of the hair, it's blonde and if I'm not mistaken it is the girl."

Up in the helicopter above the monument, Julie was half hanging out of it trying to zoom into the top of the monument, it was risky but it was the only way of seeing where the clue was. She told the pilot to keep where they were as she managed to zoom into the emblem of the rocket.

She looked above it on the rim and the top of the chimney but she couldn't see anything anywhere. She shook her head in disappointment as she again zoomed into the Rocket Emblem. This time she looked beneath it and she noticed what looked like an arrow pointing downwards. She zoomed onto the wall beneath it but again she couldn't see anything. She realised that the clue, if there was one, had to be a lot further down so she asked the pilot to go lower.

Down below them in their hotel room the Lord and Joseph were still watching as the helicopter hovered just above the hill by the side of the chimney. "The bastards lied in that letter," Gabriel cried as he got a better view of the copter to confirm that it was Julie. "They never found the clue, it couldn't have been on the top otherwise they wouldn't have flown down to the hill."

"Yes, but now they must have it," Joseph replied. "And that must mean that the clue is on the bottom, so if they could find it then why not us."

"Come on lad," Gabriel told him as he grabbed his coat. "Let's get back up there and check again."

Back in the helicopter, Julie had given up looking for it, she hadn't found anything at all but at least she knew where the clue was, it was mixed up on the bottom pediment with all the other graffiti. She gave the helicopter pilot a nod and he started to fly back to his base in Welshpool.

Within an hour, Gabriel and Joseph had made their way up to the monument. Gabriel had brought his binoculars with him so that he could inspect the walls of the chimney. After not finding anything on the chimney, they began to look on the lower pediment, it was full of graffiti but nothing of which they could make any sense of.

They didn't have a starting point; their binoculars weren't powerful enough to reach up to the emblem of the Rocket so they didn't know what part of the pediment to inspect closely. They ended up taking photographs of every part of the pediment and going back to their hotel where Joseph could dissect every part of the pediment for any minute detail of the clue. It would be slow progress for he would have to separate all the modern graffiti from the older etchings, but eventually, he felt that he would find the etching that came from the nineteenth century.

An excited Julie told Alex where she thought the clue might be as soon as she left the copter and they quickly set off back to Aberystwyth before the darkness of night arrived. They arrived back on Pen Dinas early evening and as they looked up the monument they followed the chimney down from the Rocket emblem to the lower pediment.

On looking over the pediment, they decided that here was where the clue should be. The top of the pediment was caked in graffiti, graffiti from all ages. They decided to look for the oldest etchings, there were some that stood out but nothing that they could make out to be a clue. As the sun began to set, they hurriedly took some photos of the etchings so that they could look them over more closely in the comfort of their hotel room.

As the darkness of night drew over, they were back in the Hafod Arms Hotel desperately trying to drag the clue out from over a hundred and fifty years of graffiti.

"The only thing that it could be was that there," Julie told him as she enlarged the image on her laptop.

"It's not complete though," Alex replied as he tried to zoom in closer. "That's about the best I can get it, it goes all blurry if I enlarge it anymore."

"It has to be that," Julie cried. "That's the oldest etching on the pediment, but what could it mean?"

"Obviously, A B C must mean Arthur's Burial Chamber or Cavern," Alex told her. "I suppose R V R means a River, but which river and what the hell does DOG GR mean, there's obviously some letters missing."

"There's one definitely missing after the G," Julie replied as she pointed to the decay between the G and the GR, but GR we haven't got a clue how long that word was because of the damage to the pediment. It could be the name of the town where the river runs through, but which town."

Alex reached for his A to Z of Wales and read through the towns and villages that began with DO "There're loads that begin with DO," he told her. "But only one that has a GR for the 4th and 5th letter, Dol-gran in Carmarthenshire."

"Find the page and see if there's a river and a mountain nearby?" Julie asked excitedly.

Alex turned to page 45 and checked section 2-D where he found the village of Dol-gran. "Yes," he cried. "It has a river and it was in the middle of the mountains."

"We've found it then," she shouted. "We've found Arthur's mountain."

"It can't be," Alex whispered disappointedly.

"What do you mean?" Julie asked him. "It has to be there."

Alex shook his head and showed her where Carmarthenshire was on the map "It's in South Wales," he told her. "There's no way that it was the right mountain, Concerve definitely mentioned that they were looking for a passage through the mountains to Porthmadog, Dol-gran was nowhere near and besides there are many closer ports to their than Porthmadog."

After again looking at the maps, Julie finally agreed that they had reached the wrong conclusion, they would have to check again and see if any of the names around Snowdonia and the Cambrian Mountains matched up to anything on the pediment but nothing stood out so they gave up for the night and went to bed.

The next day after again checking the monument without success Julie left Alex in the Hafod Arms Hotel while she drove into Aberystwyth to see if the library held any old photographs of the lower pediment before the decay set in. Meanwhile, a short walk away from the library was the Belle Vue Royal Hotel on Marine Terrace where Gabriel and Joseph were still staying.

The Belle Vue was situated on the old Victorian Promenade and the front of the hotel had a stunning view over Cardigan Bay. That was where Gabriel was stood leaning over the bar ordering himself another whisky.

"Isn't it too early to be boozing?" Joseph asked as he eventually traced where Gabriel had disappeared to.

"Never too early for a drink," Gabriel replied. "You should try it, it might bring you out of your shell a bit."

"I don't need a drink to wake me up and neither do you, you know what the doctor said."

"Screw the doctors, what do they know."

"They know more than you and they said if you carried on drinking to excess then you'll die."

"We all die sooner or later, besides what's left for me; my dreams for my family were, are they? I'll tell you where in blooming tatters that's where."

"It's never over till the fat lady sings," Joseph told him as he threw his arm over his shoulder. "There has to be another clue, it's just a case of waiting for that couple to use their laptop and then bingo we have them."

"They haven't used it yet, and for all, we know they may already have the damn thing."

"They may be like us, maybe the clue was there but they couldn't decipher it either, so all we have to do is to go over it again until something crops up."

"We've been over it," Gabriel shouted. "Again and again and again and still nothing, it's over lad and the sooner you except that then we can get back to our lives."

"And what life is that, watching you drink yourself into an early grave."

"My choice lad, and if you're not joining me then piss off, you're no bloody use to me anyway."

For a second, Joseph just stood there facing the Lord shaking his head, he was deeply hurt by what Gabriel had said to him, so he decided to leave the Lord to his drinking and went for a walk around the village.

He decided to try his luck in the local betting shop but everything he bet on went down and his mood didn't improve when two of the shop's customers started niggling him.

"Hey, Ginge," one of the men shouted over to him. "Where's your boyfriend today?"

"Yeah, matchstick," his mate shouted. "Where's your sugar daddy?"

"I'm not queer," Joseph shouted back.

"Still in the closet then," the first guy whispered as he tapped his mate in the chest with his elbow.

"Don't be ashamed," the second guy told him. "For you do make a nice couple."

"Screw you," Joseph shouted as he pushed past the two laughing men on his way out of the bookmakers.

Julie had no luck in the library so she set off back to Alex, as she walked over to her black Vauxhall Corsa she didn't see the tall ginger-haired man who had just stepped out of the betting shop.

But Joseph saw her. He couldn't believe his luck he had just had the worst day of his life in the bookies, lost everything bar his shirt and who was in front of him. The woman who was responsible for his only friend in the world going back on the booze, well he'd teach her not to upset his friend.

He hurriedly crossed the road to catch up to her before she could reach the safety of her car. Julie didn't see Joseph cross the road and as she opened the car door and got in Joseph jumped into the passenger side. "Don't think about getting out," he told her as he held Gabriel's small pistol into her side. "Thought you got shut of us did you?" he asked as she stared at him in horror.

"What do you want?" she asked as she desperately looked around her for help.

"What do you think?" he replied. "The next clue of course."

"There wasn't one?"

"Yeah, sure, you must have found something, you didn't stop around very long in that chopper."

Julie looked at him in surprise "Didn't think we'd twig eh!" he told her. "Who else but you two would circle the chimney that closes, there must have

103

been something there however small, and I want to know what it was, the Lord wants to know what the next clue was and I'm here to make sure he does."

"You won't shoot me," Julie cried. "You need me."

Joseph shook his head "We only need one of you, I could shoot you here and put your pretty little body in the nearest ditch, your husband would just think that we have you locked up and I've seen the way you are with each other, he loves you and love will cause a man to do almost anything."

"He won't tell you a thing without confirmation that I'm alive. Remember the man who thinks he holds all the cards holds nothing if he doesn't have the ace."

"What the hell was that?" Joseph asked her. "Well, honey the ace is here in my hands," he lifted the gun up and pressed it underneath her left breast."

"Is that the way you get your thrills?" she whispered. "Molesting women under gunpoint."

"I don't need a gun," he shouted as he whacked her in the face with his right elbow breaking her nose on the spot. "Here," he cried as he pulled out a cloth. "Stem the bleeding with that."

"You bastard," she whispered as she snorted clots of blood into his face and tried to get out of the car.

"No, you don't bitch," he cried as he dragged her back into the car. "Try to be clever again and I'll—"

"You'll what?" Julie screamed. "Hit me again, well come on freak hit me, show what a great man you are."

Joseph calmly looked around him, for the main road in a town centre there weren't many shoppers around. He looked again and when he was sure that no one was watching "Don't call me a freak," he shouted as he punched her full strength in her face. He wasn't really a fighting man so he didn't really know the power that he had in his fists, the only thing that he was aware of was that she was quiet now, too quiet.

"Why wouldn't you just tell me?" he cried as he lifted up her blood-splattered chin and held her face to his. "All you had to do was answer me, but no you wouldn't would you? You had to be clever, didn't you? Now, look what you made me do? All these years I've been good and now you went and dragged me back where I was before, you're just like all the rest, you're the freaks, not me."

As the blood flowed down her face, he began to panic, the road had suddenly become much busier and it was only a matter of time before somebody noticed Julie's blood-splattered face and sweater.

He had no choice he had to drive the car away, but first, he had to swap places with her. So he calmly opened his car door and quickly rushed around the car to the driver's side. As some shoppers walked past the car chatting, he stood in front of the driver's window whistling patience by taking that.

Once the path was clear, he opened the driver's door and shoved her limp body over into the passenger seat and then placed himself in the driver's chair and drove off out of the town and into the surrounding countryside.

When he felt that he had found a safe place to stop he lifted Julie's body up out of the car and carried it into the woods. The blood was still pouring from her nose but on checking her over he realised that she was still breathing. He needed to find something to stem the flow of blood but what? He was only wearing shorts and a red sleeveless vest.

He looked down at Julie's body; she had on a tight white sweater that was now ladened with blood and a thin blue skirt. He carefully lifted up her back and pulled her sweater off leaving her lying there with just her blue bra on. He stood on the sweater and pulled it until he managed to rip some shreds of it and then proceeded to wipe her face down and then he held a piece over her nose, until finally, the flow of bleeding stopped.

He then sighed with relief as she started to come through. As she opened her eyes, she witnessed him ripping more shreds from her blue skirt which he had now taken off her. He was using these shreds to gag and bound her before placing her in the boot of her own car. "You look ever so sexy in your sky blue undies," he laughed as she stared up at him. "Only wished that I had more time, and then I'll show you what I can do with a gun."

He held the gun down to her thighs and rubbed it between her legs. "Once I get the clue, my lady, I will have me some fun, believe me, I will, but for now my beauty it's time for bo-bo's." Julie heard him laughing as he slammed the boot shut.

After wiping the bloodstains from the car windscreen and seats, he drove the car back to the Belle Vue Royal Hotel to show Gabriel his prize. He found Gabriel propping up the bar and dragged him outside the hotel to proudly show him what he had in the car boot. As he opened the boot, Gabriel noticed an unusual look upon Joseph's face, it was a look of supreme pride as if what he had in the boot was the most precious procession in the world.

"What have you done?" Gabriel cried as he saw Julie tied up in the boot, wearing just her underwear.

"Found her in town," a smug Joseph replied.

"Is she dead?"

"No, just tired that's all."

"Where's all the blood from?"

"She wouldn't behave, so I hit her," laughed Joseph.

"You know I don't work that way Joseph, why did you hit her?"

Joseph looked up to the lord and then smiled as he looked down to Julie "I thought you'd be happy," he replied. "I thought if I brought her here we could force the next clue out of her hubbie, and then you'd have a reason not to drink, the doctor told you not to drink, they said that your heart wasn't strong enough to cope with how you get when you drink."

"Joseph, what have you done?"

"I did it for you," Joseph cried. "I did it for you."

"We need to get her to a hospital quick, she needs help."

"Can't let you do that, sir," Joseph told him as he slammed the boot shut. "They'll put me away again like they did the last time, I'm not going back there, they do things to me."

"It'll be alright son," Gabriel whispered. "They'll understand; you didn't mean it; it was an accident; they'll understand."

"Yeah," Joseph cried. "They'll understand like they understood the last time, it was an accident then but they didn't understand did they, they put me away."

A look of shock came over the Lord's face as he looked into Joseph's dead eyes "But you were innocent weren't you, you told me that you never touched that young girl."

"She was teasing me," Joseph shouted. "They were all teasing me, she called me a freak, I'm not a freak, they made me a freak, so I showed them, I showed them what a freak could do, I snapped her neck, I didn't mean to. She called me a freak so I grabbed her before I knew it she was dead, I didn't know my own strength."

"What did you do?" Gabriel calmly asked him.

"I buried her in the graveyard, I found an unused grave, next day it got used she'll never be found," a smiling Joseph told him.

106

"Joseph," Gabriel whispered. "Joseph you have to tell me, what grave you buried her in, her family would still be pining for her."

"Family," Joseph snorted. "Don't talk to me about family, my family disowned me, they knew what a freak I was."

"Joseph you're not a freak, come with me, I can help you."

"No one can help me, not now," Joseph shouted as he shoved the Lord to the ground.

"Joseph," Gabriel shouted as he saw Joseph speed off down the road.

Gabriel picked himself up and reached for his phone to call the police but as it rang he hung off and put his phone away. He realised that if he got the police involved then Joseph would most probably kill the girl and then himself. At this point, he was more concerned about Julie's safety than Joseph's.

The only thing he could think of was to try to find Alex and maybe together they could track Joseph down. He hoped against hope that they were still staying at the Hafod Arms Hotel near the bridge, so he set off immediately for there.

Chapter Seven

The Final Clue

The base of
The Wellington Monument

Somewhere along the A44 Joseph had run out of petrol so he opened the car boot and dragged a now conscious Julie out of the car and was dragging her through the woodlands. After about half an hour, they reached the Devil's Bridge and there he had a thought, they could both hide underneath the bridge but he needed a rope. He took the gag from her over her mouth and asked her where the rope was.

"Screw you," she shouted.

"Where's the God damn rope?" he screamed as he slapped her across the face. She looked back at him and spat blood into his face. "Think you're funny do you?" he cried as he grabbed her by the neck. "Well, laugh at this." He lifted her face up and repeatedly punched her in it then held her against the bridge and started to throttle her against the decaying brickwork. "Where's the fucking rope?" he shouted. "Believe me, I will throw you over, now where's the fucking rope?"

"What do you want it for?" she asked him. "We can't exactly tie it to the top there'll be people in the shops above."

"That's why we are going to crawl along the side of the bridge; you've got small enough fingers to grip it with."

"That's impossible, we'll fall."

"Maybe you will, but I'm confident that I'll make it, don't worry I'm quite strong if you fall I'll pull you up, but piss me about and I'll shoot you on the spot, think about calling for help and I'll shoot you and whoever comes to your aid, believe me, at this point, I'll do anything to keep you quiet, now where's the bloody rope." He again gripped her by her throat "Last chance honey, where's the rope?"

As she battled for breath, she nodded over to the bushes by the end of the bridge. "Good girl," he said as he smiled at her. "Now stay there," he laughed as she fell to the floor. He quickly retrieved the rope and tied it around the thickest tree he could find and tied the other end securely around Julie's half-naked body.

He then wrapped the middle of the rope around his waist and lowered Julie down onto the ledge before slowly following her himself. They slowly and carefully made their way along the brickwork of the bridge and easily managed to reach the bottom bridge before any of the tourists above became aware of them.

"What are you going to do now?" Julie asked him. "As soon as anyone comes down those steps, they'll see us."

"I've thought about that," Joseph told her as he grabbed her by her throat and punched her in the face again and again until she blanked out. "I've told you I know what I'm doing," he whispered to her blood-splattered face as he tied and gagged her again.

As he placed her bloodied body into the damp overgrowth, he gently stroked her chin and smiled at her. "It'll be alright, girl; you'll soon be safe," he whispered to her as he kissed her battered lips. Then he sat by her side with his thumb in his mouth rocking to and though on his knees.

Outside the Hafod Arms, Gabriel took a deep breath before walking up to the entrance. How the hell can he tell Alex about his wife being kidnapped? For a second, he waited before opening the door and walking up to the receptionist and asking if Alex was still staying there. Luckily he was and the receptionist told him that he had just gone into the bar about five minutes before.

Gabriel walked over to the bar and looked through the glass door. He could see Alex just taking a seat in the beer garden. He took another deep breath then opened the door and walked over to where Alex was sat. Alex was surprised to see Gabriel stood before him and he wasn't prepared for what the Lord was about to tell him.

"You're joking, he's done what?" Alex cried on hearing about Julie.

"Calm down, she seemed okay."

"Okay," Alex shouted. "My wife's been kidnapped by a flaming maniac and you say it's okay, we have to call the police."

"We can't," Gabriel told him. "He's too unstable there's no telling what he might do, I should have seen it coming. Why didn't I see it coming?"

"Shit!" Alex cried. "It's like Allen all over again."

"Who's Allen?"

"A guy from my hometown down south," Alex told him. "We got involved with him while we were after The Rainhill Trials, he blamed me for." Alex paused a while and looked up to the dark cloudy sky and smiled "Something, so he kidnapped Julie."

"What happened?"

"Well, to be honest, he didn't actually get Julie, he had only met her once so he got mixed up and grabbed her mate by mistake," Alex stopped talking and took a sip of his beer before continuing. "He killed her, shot her in her back, he's now inside for life, hopefully, if life now means life," He took another sip from his glass "But it was just the same then I couldn't go to the police."

"There's a chance that if I get to face him I could talk him down," Gabriel told him.

"A chance," Alex replied. "How much of a chance?"

"It's slim but I'm the only one he'd listen to."

Alex drank his beer up and stood up "Right then let's get going."

"I think he would have headed out into the country," Gabriel cried as they ran to his car. "He doesn't like crowded places."

"What kind of nutters do you employ?"

"He seemed normal, and I didn't know about the girl he killed until today."

"What girl?" Alex cried. "You mean he's killed before?"

"A long time ago," Gabriel replied. "But he told me he was innocent and now this morning he claimed he killed her."

"Charming," Alex cried. "And now he's got my wife half-naked in the boot of his car."

As they drove along the A44, Gabriel filled Alex in with all that Joseph had said about the young girl's death.

"Over there in that ditch," Alex cried as he spotted his black Corsa dumped by the side of the road.

They screeched to a halt and ran over to the abandoned car. "Nothing," Alex cried as the boot was bare. "Where does this road go to?"

Gabriel grabbed his map and pinpointed their position on it "We're here and there is the Devil's bridge."

At the exact moment, he said Devil's Bridge the dark sky opened above them and the heavens opened and a vicious thunderstorm began. They ran back to the safety of the car and set off to the bridge.

"I hope to God that he's got her under shelter," Alex cried as he watched the rain bounce off the car bonnet as they drove.

"Aye," Gabriel replied. "It won't do much good if she's caught in this."

At the Devil's bridge, the two shops had decided to shut up for the day, no tourists will come in this weather and if they did they didn't need any assistant in entering the turnstiles. Underneath the bottom bridge, Joseph had just noticed the rope swinging in the wind and realised that it was a giveaway to where he was hiding so he decided to brave the elements and climb up it and hide the rope in the bushes again.

"There's the bridge," Alex told the Lord. "Park here, we'll go the rest on foot then if he was on the bridge he wouldn't hear us coming."

Gabriel agreed and stopped the car. As soon as he parked up, Alex got out and ran up to the bridge. Joseph meanwhile had just reached the safety of the ledge, he was drenched through, he was only wearing shorts and a tee-shirt and he could barely see in this down power. He kept wiping the rain from his face as he struggled to untie the rope from the tree. As he finally got it loose, he could see a blurry figure walking down the steps towards him.

He wiped the water from his eyes to see Alex stood before him with Gabriel struggling behind.

"Keep back," Joseph told him as he pulled out the small pistol.

"What have you done to her?" Alex cried through the wind and the rain. "Where is she?"

Joseph smiled and nodded over the railings "Down there."

Alex ran over to the rail and looked down into the ravine "You've dropped her!" he cried. "You've pushed her over."

"Relax," Joseph told him. "She's not dead; well I don't think she is."

"Where is she then?"

"Where we left you both together day and if you stayed there then none of this would have happened, this was all your fault, why didn't you stay put?"

"Give me the rope," Alex shouted.

Joseph looked down at the rope he was holding in his left hand "You want this; I thought you were scared of heights?"

"My wife's down there."

"My complements there me old son," Joseph replied. "She's got a cracking body, just a pity I didn't have the time to use it."

"You bastard I'll."

"You'll what," Joseph cried. "Take a good look, who's holding the gun sunshine."

"Joseph," Gabriel cried as he finally reached them both. "Give me the gun."

"Stay out of this, sir," Joseph told his former employer. "It's between him and me, we're kind of in the middle of something here, he wants me to give him the rope but I want to drop it over the bridge."

"Joseph," spoke Gabriel calmly. "We need the rope to reach her; she'll die down there in this weather."

"Better here than me," Joseph cried. "She deserves to, she called me a freak and I'm not a flaming freak."

"No," shouted Alex. "Just a total nut job."

"Alex, stay out of this," Gabriel shouted as Joseph held the rope over the edge. "Joseph, don't let another girl die, I can help you, we can both help you, I have money I can take you where you want, he won't report you, he'll let you go free, but we need to help the girl."

"You won't report me?" Joseph asked Alex.

"If she's okay then what harm have you done," Alex shouted back through the howling wind. "Listen to Gabriel, he can help you."

"He won't press charges?" Joseph asked Gabriel.

"Why should he," Gabriel replied. "If the girl is alright, no harm has been done, there's still time to change what you have done."

"I didn't mean it," Joseph cried. "I thought it'll help you, I thought if I helped you, you'd stop drinking, you shouldn't drink, the doctor told you not to drink, you'll die."

Alex looked over to Gabriel "Bad heart that's all," Gabriel told him. "Come on lad, pass me the gun, you'll be fine I promise."

"I'll be fine?" Joseph asked him as he looked down at Gabriel who was slowly walking towards him with his arms open as if to hug him.

As Gabriel got within arm's reach of him, he reached for the gun and in the melee that followed it went off and Gabriel fell to the ground.

"What have I done?" Joseph cried as he looked down to Gabriel lying on the floor with blood leaking through his shirt.

"You stupid get," Alex shouted. "You shot him; you shot the only guy who could help you."

"I didn't mean to," Joseph cried. "This is all your fault, you killed him."

"Don't be so flaming stupid," Alex shouted as he knelt down on the flooded path to help Gabriel.

"Get away from him," Joseph cried as he kicked Alex away from Gabriel. "Leave him alone."

"Don't be a fool," Alex shouted as he looked up at him. "He needs help, he'll die."

"It's too late for him now," Joseph cried. "For him, for me, you and her down there, it's all too late."

"Joseph, no!" Alex shouted as Joseph threw the rope over the edge.

Alex picked himself up and ran to the edge and looked over to see through the swirling rain the rope dropping down to the river 300 feet below them "Why?" Alex asked as he threw his arms up in the air. "Why drop it, you could have saved her, it's still not too late, we need to phone for help."

"Put down your phone or I'll…"

"You'll what," Alex shouted. "You'll shoot me, well go on the big boy, flaming shoot me, I mean what have I got to live for if you won't let me save her."

"If that's what you want," Joseph told him as he lifted the gun up to Alex's head. "Then so be it."

Just as he was about to pull the trigger Joseph heard a groan from by his feet. It was Gabriel, he was still alive. "Sir," Joseph cried as he looked down at him. Sensing his chance Alex charged at Joseph knocking him into the metal railings. Joseph dropped the gun and they both tumbled to the ground wrestling through the puddles of rain that had formed in the many potholes on the floor of the footpath.

It wasn't much of a contest for Joseph was clearly the much taller, bigger and stronger of the two. He easily overpowered his much smaller opponent and gripped him by his neck and was holding him by the edge trying to force him over. Alex was kicking for his life but no matter how hard he kicked and clawed at Joseph, Joseph ignored it and finally forced Alex over the edge.

Alex was dangling over the edge of the 300 feet drop to clear death but he wasn't giving up without a fight, he wrapped his arms around Joseph's neck and was clinging on for dear life. Joseph was pounding his fists into Alex's head and body desperately trying to weaken him into losing his grip. Eventually, Alex could take no more and his arms slipped from Joseph's neck and he fell downwards frantically grasping hold of an outgrown tree with his right hand.

In this downpour, it took a couple of seconds for Joseph to see that Alex hadn't fallen to his death but was clinging on with his arms wrapped around an old outgrown tree. Joseph smiled down at him and then placed his foot onto Alex's arm and started to press down hard onto it, twisting his heel into the arm while reaching over the edge and reigning punch after punch onto the top of Alex's head.

Just as he was about to give up a shot rang out and Joseph stopped punching and tumbled over the edge and dropped down into the ravine, his body bouncing off the rocky sides eventually becoming lodged between the thinnest parts of the rocky chasm.

Alex looked up to see Gabriel shuffling his wounded body up to the edge of the bridge with the pistol in his hand. Alex smiled with relief and pulled himself up and onto the safety of the ledge and knelt down to see to the Lord.

"You shot him," Alex cried. "You killed him."

"Aye," Gabriel spluttered. "Had to, he had changed that lad, that wasn't the lad I brought in from the cold, that was a damn bad lot that was."

"What about you, are you alright?" Alex asked as he noticed the blood flowing through his white shirt.

"Forget about me," Gabriel told him. "See to her down there, she needs you more than ever now."

"Shit! You're right " Alex cried as he picked himself up and looked over the bridge. "Julie," he shouted. "Julie can you hear me."

"She won't hear you in this wind," Gabriel shouted.

"Your right, but at least it's stopped bloody raining at last."

"Use my phone," Gabriel shouted. "Call for help."

"It might be too late," Alex told him. "I have to go down there for her."

"Don't be foolish, you'll slip, everything's damn wet."

"I've no choice," Alex replied. "She may not last for much longer and if she died when I could have saved her then I'd never forgive myself, I'm going down, use the phone for yourself; hopefully, I'll see you soon, if not I'll meet you in hell"

As Alex walked towards the ledge, he saw the gun lying on the floor so he picked it up "Don't want any kids to find that," he told the lord as he shoved it down the back of his pants. He looked over the edge and tried to fathom out how Julie climbed up from the lower bridge. Each way he looked it looked too dangerous, but he noticed that from the steep path by the left of the bridge there seemed to be a small ledge that stretched out from the overgrowth. It led out underneath the original bridge.

"If I can reach that ledge," he cried to the injured Lord. "Then maybe I could climb up the brickwork of the old bridge and reach her that way, at least I wouldn't be looking down."

He helped the lord up and through the turnstile before going back down the slippery path towards the bottom of the Devil's Bridge. Once down, he slowly and carefully made his way through the damp overgrown weeds and onto the small rocky ledge.

He slowly moved along the ledge carefully lifting his feet over the outgrowing roots of the trees that had grown out of the brickwork over the last century or so. Once he was clear of all the greenery, he backed against the wall of the middle bridge and inched his way to the wall of the oldest bridge. When he reached the safety of the decaying brickwork he crouched down and wormed his way over to the edge to check how secure the ledge was where he would have to place his feet to start his climb.

It looked worse than it was, the ledge was about 8 feet thick and there wasn't any of it coming loose. He managed to get back to the safety of the wall without getting a glimpse of the 300 feet drop. He leant backwards into the wall and lifted his head upwards and shouted "Julie, Julie, can you hear me, it's me Alex, I'm down here, can you hear me."

He started to panic when he didn't hear a reply so without thinking about the danger to himself he began to climb up the wall of the bridge. Slowly at first, slowly and carefully but the more finger holds he found, the more confidence ran through him and before he had time to worry about the height he reached the top of the wall.

As he pulled himself up, he saw his wife's body dumped amongst the weeds that had grown over the years. "Julie," he cried as he scurried over to her half-naked body. "Are you okay? Give me a sign, just one sign." As he lifted up her head, he heard a faint groan come from her. She was still alive but she wouldn't be for much longer if he didn't get her up to safety.

He took off his shirt and wrapped it around her to keep her warm. Tears came to his eyes as he cradled her in his arms "How could he do this?" he sobbed as he looked at her battered and bruised face. "How could anyone harm you, my dear?" He whispered to her face as he wiped the dried blood from under her nose. "Why would he do this? What possessed him into doing this, the bastard, well he won't be hurting anyone else, my love."

The next moment, he heard the wailing of the sirens above him. He smiled as he realised that Gabriel must have managed to phone for help. "Don't worry darling; you'll soon be safe; help's arrived. You'll be safe and warm soon, hang on, my love; please hang on."

He crawled over to the edge and lay on his back to look upwards "DOWN HERE," he shouted. "We're down here; we need help, down here."

Up above him on the top bridge Gabriel had passed out and the medics were knelt by his side checking him over and giving him some much-needed oxygen. They had no idea that Alex and Julie were two bridges below them. They were a tad confused about who had phoned the ambulance and had left the Lord alone out in the middle of nowhere.

Down below Alex was starting to get worried, he had realised that if Gabriel was unconscious then no one would know they were beneath him. He reached into his pocket and pulled out his mobile desperately hoping that it hadn't got damaged while he was fighting with Joseph. Luckily it was in good working order but he struggled to pick up a signal on it. "Blasted cheap phone," he shouted as the reception kept cutting out.

"Thank God," he sighed as he heard a voice on the other end. He explained to the receptionist what his problem was and where he was and for a minute the line went dead, until finally, the woman returned to the line.

"Hello can you hear me?" she asked. "Can you repeat where you are because the Ambulance has arrived on the bridge and was treating the injured party?"

"I'm on the Devil's Bridge," Alex cried. "My wife needs help, tell them where we are."

"Sir, the ambulance men are on the bridge, where are you?"

"I'm underneath them, I'm on the old bridge, under them, tell them where I am."

"Sir, I can't understand you, you keep breaking up."

"Bugger it," Alex shouted as he threw his phone down and pulled out the gun from the back of his pants. "Hear this, you bastards," he shouted as he fired the gun twice into the air.

That worked, the medics heard the shots and carefully peered over the edge and one of them heard Alex's cry for help. "Hang on, sir," the medic shouted. "We'll try to come down to you." They placed Gabriel into the back of the ambulance and then made their way down the steep path to get onto the level ground with Alex.

On hearing that, Julie was desperately ill one of the medics tried to climb up to them but he wasn't much of a climber and kept losing his grip, the final time almost falling into the ravine. They shouted up to Alex that it wasn't safe for them to try again so the only way that they could reach them was by calling out the mountain rescue.

Alex left them to their call and shuffled back under the bridge to try to keep Julie warm until help finally arrived. Less than half an hour later help did arrive in the shape of a mountain rescue helicopter which winched them both up to safety.

As they flew to the nearest hospital, Alex kept hold of Julie's hand and was whispering to her that she'd be alright. As they flew over the National Library of Wales in Aberystwyth, the rescue helicopter began to descend and it landed on the grounds of the Bronglais General Hospital where Julie was whisked through the emergency entrance. Within half an hour of them being winched off the bridge, they were all in the warmth and safety of the hospital.

After reassurances from the doctors that Julie would be alright, Alex went to the ward facing to see how Gabriel was. He didn't like or trust him but he felt that he owed him because he had saved his life on more than one occasion. He wasn't allowed to see Gabriel but was told that the gunshot merely grazed his shoulder.

The doctors were more concerned about his heart, it had stopped a couple of times on the journey to the hospital but he appeared to be growing stronger by the minute. Alex was told that maybe tomorrow he would be strong enough to take in a visitor.

There was nothing more that he could do there so he went back to the Hafod Arms to pick up some dry clothes for when Julie was fully recovered, which he hoped wouldn't be too long. That night in his bed was one of the worse he had ever had in his life. It didn't feel right being by himself, he had only been with Julie for just under two years but in that time they had never been apart and he felt that part of him was missing that night.

The next morning he went back to the hospital where he was relieved to find Julie almost back to her chirpy self. Apart from breaking her nose, Joseph didn't do much real harm to her, a load of bruising over her chest, shoulders and face but once they had reset her nose she would be allowed to go home. While the surgeon set her nose Alex went to visit Gabriel who had also come through his own private battle with his weak heart.

He was still weak but he was able to recognise Alex and he had full memory of what Joseph had done. He told Alex that he was sorry for everything that they had done to them, even excepting the blame for killing Alex's two cars.

Alex just smiled at him and told him to take it easy. But as he was leaving Gabriel called him back in and gave him the key to his room in the Belle Vue Royal, which was only down the road. He told him that under the bed was a small black suitcase and it contained everything that his family had collected over the last 150 years about Arthur's Gold Mine.

Alex told him that they may as well forget about it because they had run out of clues and turned to walk out of the room. Gabriel pulled him by the arm back to the bed and whispered "You have a better brain than me maybe you can find something that I missed."

"We've looked at everything with any connection to Arthur and his burial chamber and come back with nothing," Alex replied.

"Please," Gabriel begged him. "Have a look, just a quick peep and then if you don't spot anything then give up."

"Well," Alex replied. "I suppose I'm going to have to go to your hotel to tell them about you and Joseph anyway so I may as well have a quick look, under your bed you say in a black suitcase."

Gabriel nodded as Alex left the room to go back to Julie.

Alex waited nearly an hour for Julie to come out of surgery but on seeing her he was downhearted to hear that she had to spend another night in the hospital because her blood pressure was too high. He kissed her goodbye and told her that he'd pop back to see her in the evening as he had to go to inform Gabriel's hotel about what had happened to him.

When he arrived at the Belle Vue Royal he asked to see the manager. On telling him about Joseph dying and Gabriel being hospitalised, he was allowed to go up to Gabriel's room to get some change of clothes and some personal stuff. The personal stuff is a small black suitcase that he retrieved from under the bed.

He was going back to the hospital in the evening so he thought that he would drop off the Lord's belongings then, so he spent the afternoon in his own hotel room going through the documentation that he found in the black suitcase.

In the suitcase were 15 old maps of Wales showing different locations where the Farthingay family had searched over the last 150 years. He copied down the names of the mountains that had been searched in the hope that something stuck out.

Moel Panamnan	Moel ddu	Mynyd mawr	Yr Aran
Ygarn Cnicht	Craig Wren	Snowdon	Moe
Ysgyfawogod	Rhinog Fawr	Garnedd goch	Ydrosgl Yllethr
Tryfan Consl-y-wal	Moel	Siabod	Glder Fawr
Glyder Fach	Moel Eilio	Foel-fras	Carnod Dafyo

As he looked at them and checked them against the map of North Wales, circling each one on the map, he was stunned to find three mountains that hadn't been circled. Which was the Moel Hebog near the village of Beddgelert and two near the village of Ffestiniog Moelwyn Mawr and Moelwyn Bach.

He searched through the old files of Farthingay's and came across a piece written in 1865 saying that Stephenson wasn't a fool, he wouldn't have disturbed the gold mine by tunnelling through the mountain so he would have chosen a different route, so any mountains that had railways running through don't bother to search.

Beneath all the loose papers was an 1864 copy of the News of the World and circled on the back page was a story about Jeremiah Farthingay's death in Wales.

> On Sunday, last in the river at the side of the Pass of Aberglaslyn near the village of Beddgelert in Wales. The body of the Right Hon Jeremiah Farthingay, second son of Admiral Joseph Farthingay, was found dead with knife wounds to his back.
>
> Farthingay was married to Mary and was the father of William and Anne. It is unknown why he was found so far from where his family was residing. An inquest will be held once the family of the deceased arrived in the village.

Alex found it strange that Farthingay's body was discovered quite close to one of the mountains that he claimed not to have any interest in, and he thought it was worth it to check out the mountain range of Beddgelert. The more he read of Farthingay's files one thing stood out.

Farthingay never mentioned Arthur or any of the artefacts after the first couple of pages, after that he only mentioned the Gold Mine or Cavern of Gold. Indeed the Farthingay's were money men as Concerve rightly observed in his journal. They weren't historians; they were only interested in money and gold.

He pulled out a modern map and checked the ones that hadn't been touched, and the one thing that they all had in common was that they all had at one time or another a railway line running through or over them. Alex realised that because they had railways around them then Farthingay automatically bypassed them obviously thinking that Stephenson wouldn't have built a railway through the mountain that Arthur's Cavern was under for the chance of it being discovered.

But then again throughout all his investigations and research into Robert Stephenson, Alex had found him to be a man of his own mind, he had the money, he had the knowledge surely it wouldn't have been too much for him to build a tunnel through the mountain and still manage to keep the cavern hidden.

The more he thought about it the more Alex got excited. It had to be, that's the reason why no one ever discovered it because Stephenson had built a bloody railway over it. Anyone who was looking for it would never have thought about looking in the one place where Stephenson was actually digging. Alex shook his head and smiled at the simplicity of it as he realised that now he had the mountain almost in his grasp.

He spent the next couple of hours on the internet doing research on the three untouched mountains. There were only two areas that clicked in his mind. The hills around Ffestiniog and Beddgelert. They were the only two that had railways that ran from Porthmadog to copper mines in the mountain range.

And both were about the same distance from the coastal town. Alex looked at them both on the map and visualised in his mind that in the nineteenth century it would have taken nearly a day's travel on horseback to reach the mines.

He couldn't wait until the evening so that he could tell Julie about his discovery. He dropped the Lord's belongings off on his way and rushed into Julie's room. He was delighted to see her sat up in bed with a smile on her face for him. He spent the next hour telling her and showing her what he had discovered.

After checking the facts over and over, Julie was convinced as well and they decided that on her release from the hospital they would drive up and check both places out to see if anything matched up to the clues they found on Pen Dinas. While they waited for the doctor to check if Julie was fit enough to leave the hospital Alex paid a visit to Gabriel to inform him of what he had found.

"You're wasting your time in Beddgelert," Gabriel told him. "I too had an inkling about that place, but I couldn't find anything and I had a load of decent surveyors working for me, there's nowt in the hills, believe me."

"What about Ffestiniog?" Alex asked. "Did you check there?"

"I'm telling you, son. Everywhere had been checked; I've checked the whole damned country from hill to hill, mountain to mountain, there's nowt there."

"You must have missed something."

"Aye, there's a chance of that, but without a meaningful clue what are we supposed to do."

"We have a clue."

"What! But you told me you never found anything."

"It's not much, but we think it's part of the clue," Alex pulled out his notebook from his pocket and showed him the photo that he took of the pediment. "We think that's the clue, but as you can see half of it is corroded."

"Let's have a look," Gabriel said as he reached for his glasses.

"See the three words," Alex asked him. "We think A B C means Arthur's Burial Chamber, R V R must mean river obviously and the bottom one must be a town, village next to the river, but there're no villages in the area around Porthmadog beginning with DOG."

"Could be a monument or something that stood by the river."

"You may have something there, but what?"

"We may never know but the only thing that we can do is believe, believe that it was out there. Search Beddgelert and Ffestiniog. See if you can find a monument, statue or even a house that begins with DOG which stood by a river."

"I will," Alex told him. "As soon as Julie gets the nod, we are going and if we find out I promise you that we won't enter the cavern until you are with us, we owe you that."

"You don't owe me anything."

"You saved mine and Julie's life without you we'd both be dead, so don't say we owe you nothing."

As Alex was leaving the room, Gabriel shouted back "Before you go lad, there's something you must know."

"What?" Alex asked.

"I've not got long in this life, I know it and if you have spoken to the doctors then you'll know it too."

"Don't talk like that, you'll be fine' you're still a young man."

"Too many years on the liquor lad, my kidneys are shot, livers shot and my heart, well what's left of it wouldn't keep a mouse alive, but I'm okay with it and that's why I want you to know that I'm not going to sulk and destroy more lives, not when I can help lives."

"What are you on about?" Alex asked. "How can you help lives?"

"Money lad," Gabriel told him. "I have money, heaps of it, but it's no use where I'm going. I've already phoned my solicitor and he's on his way."

"What are you going to do with it?" asked a curious Alex.

"I'm signing it over, all of it over to be spread between all the homeless charities around this great country of ours."

"Homeless charities?" Alex asked. "Why homeless?"

"Because of Joseph," Gabriel replied. "I know he turned out to be a bad one but I loved him, I loved him like the son I never had and if my money can stop any more desperate homeless people from causing any harm to any innocent people then I can rest easy."

"I understand," Alex told him as he shook Gabriel's hand before leaving. "Joseph wasn't your fault; he was just one of those things. Look after yourself and I promise if we find anything you'll be the first to know."

After Julie had got the all-clear, she wanted to see Gabriel tell him that she didn't hold him responsible for what Joseph did to her. On hearing Julie's heartfelt words, Gabriel thanked her and told her to look after Alex. "I envy you two you know," he told them.

"Why on earth would anyone envy us?" Julie asked him.

"You two have what I have searched for. Love, I was never blessed with such as what you two share, cherish every moment," Gabriel replied.

"Well, I guess it can't get any worse than this," Julie told him.

"Worse," Alex told her. "There's no such word as worse."

"If there's no such word," Julie snapped. "Then why do so many people say it?"

"Only Northerners like you, my love," Alex replied as he kissed her on her forehead. "We southerners can speak properly."

"We can't all speak with a plum in our mouth?" Julie laughed.

"Where she comes from," Alex told Gabriel. "All they eat is black pudding downed by pints of bitter."

"There's nowt wrong with a tad of homeliness," Gabriel laughed as he bid them farewell.

On leaving the hospital, they made their way back to the Hafod Arms to pick up their stuff and check out before setting off to Ffestiniog. As they left the hotel, they stopped off by the Devil's Bridge. They left the car and walked over to the railings and peered over. "I can't believe you climbed down there for me," Julie told him as she clasped his hand and looked admiringly into his face. "You must love me after all."

"More than life itself," Alex replied.

"Were you not scared; after all, it's quite high."

"To be honest I walked down the path and climbed up to you."

"How did you get to the wall?"

"See that small ledge there?" he replied as he pointed down to the small path he made as he climbed through the overgrowth. "I made my way over that and backed against the wall, after that I didn't have to look down I kept my eyes up and focused on the bridge."

"My hero," she cried as she kissed him again before they saluted the bridge goodbye and went back to their car.

They set off along the A44 and then joined the A487 coast road that took them to the village of Machynlleth where they stopped for a bit of lunch. After they had eaten, they made their way to the village of Dolgellau and joined the A470 that took them through the Snowdonia National Park. After a two-hour journey along a forever winding mountain road, they finally reached the slate mine village of Ffestiniog.

Ffestiniog is a community in Gwynedd in Wales, containing Several villages, particular the settlements of Llan Ffestiniog and Blaenau Ffestiniog. Ffestiniog was a parish in Cantref Ardudwy, in 1284 Ardudwy became part of the county of Meirionnydd which became an administrative county in 1888. The village's main source of income was from the slate quarry's that surrounds the village.

They spent a couple of hours driving around the hills and slate mines of the village without finding anything that matched up with the clue that they had. They eventually found the local library and checked the local records, but again nothing matched up. They decided that Arthur's Cavern wasn't to be found around the hills of Ffestiniog so they set off for the Snowdonia National Park, and after another hour's drive along the A4085, they reached the village of Beddgelert.

Beddgelert is a village in the Snowdonia area of Gwynedd in North Wales. It is reputed to be named after the hound of legend Gelert. The village is a significant tourist attraction, its picturesque bridge crossing the River Colwyn just upstream of its confluence with the River Glaslyn. It is also the nearest village to the scenic Glaslyn gorge, an area of tumultuous river running between steep wooded hills.

On arriving in the village, they parked up in a car park just before an ice cream shop. After leaving the car, they walked along the small but busy road. They were surprised at how small the village was, if they would have carried on driving they would have passed through it within a couple of minutes. It was small but it was busy they had to walk on the road to avoid bumping into the endless stream of tourists, most of them with dogs on leads taking up most of the pavements.

As they passed a small souvenir shop, the road entered a sharp bend that took in a bridge that crossed the shallow river. They decided to cross the road and walk along the right-hand side of the river where most of the tourists were coming from.

Chapter Eight
Aberglasylyn

While Julie refreshed herself in the ladies Alex had a look at the notice board by the side of the small river. Once Julie had joined him, he showed her the local map on the notice board and pointed to where they were.

"If we follow that path just before the bridge it will lead us towards that old church," he told her as they walked towards a small bridge that crossed the river. "There may be something in the graveyard that stood out."

"You mean part of the clue or something?" she asked.

"I don't know but maybe we can find a starting point."

"Well, it was at the base of that mountain," she replied. "You never know we may get lucky."

He grabbed her hand and helped her over the stile and into the field that led them to the old church. As they walked through a flock of sheep, they noticed a small mound at the other end of the field that had been fenced off.

"What's that over there?" she cried. "Next to the remains of the old barn."

"Don't know," Alex replied. "But there seemed to be quite a few tourists by it, let's have a ramble over."

"Looks like a grave or something," Julie told him as they could see an engraving by the side of the mould.

"It's a grave of a dog," Alex told her as they reached the top of the path to see a small gravestone in the middle of a plot surrounded by a small 3 feet fence.

GELERT'S GRAVE
IN THE THIRTEENTH CENTURY, LLEWELYN, PRINCE OF
NORTH WALES, HAD A PALACE AT BEDDGELERT
ONE DAY HE WENT HUNTING WITHOUT GELERT
THE FAITHFULL HOUND
WHO WAS UNACCOUNTABLY ABSENT

ON LLEWELYN'S RETURN THE TRUANT, STAINED
AND SMEARED WITH BLOOD, JOYFULLY SPRANG
TO MEET HIS MASTER. THE PRINCE ALARMED
HASTENED TO FIND HIS SON, AND SAW THE
INFANT'S COT EMPTY, THE BEDCLOTHES AND
FLOOR COVERED WITH BLOOD.
THE FRANTIC FATHER PLUNGED HIS SWORD INTO
THE HOUND'S SIDE, THINKING IT HAD KILLED HIS
HEIR. THE DOG'S DYING YELL WAS ANSWERED BY
A CHILD'S CRY. LLEWELYN SEARCHED AND DIS-
COVERED HIS BOY UNHARMED, BUT NEARBY LAY
THE BODY OF A MIGHTY WOLF WHICH GELERT HAD
SLAIN. THE PRINCE FILLED WITH REMORSE IS SAID
NEVER TO HAVE SMILED AGAIN.
HE BURIED GELERT HERE.

"My God, that's sad," Julie cried as she grasped hold of Alex's hand. "Would you ever smile again if out happened to me?"

"My love, if you go I will follow, you know that," Alex replied as he kissed her hand. "Besides who else could I find to make me travel all over Britain in search of artefacts that may or may not exist."

"Charming," she replied.

"You know I love you though," Alex told her as he held her hand to his heart. "To be honest I wouldn't want to live without you, my world would be empty without you in it."

She smiled as she grabbed his hand and led him into the remains of Llewellyn's cottage. All it was four dry stone walls with a doorway into it. A smile came over their faces as they almost walked into a metal statue of the prince's dog Gelert that was stood by the doorway. There was nothing of interest in there for them so their attention again went over to the old church.

As they leant on the stone wall, they saw the smoke from a steam train that chugged along the line facing them on the other side of the river. They watched as it passed through a trio of tunnels that had been dug through the mountain "Bloody hell," Julie cried. "From where we are stood you could just imagine that we are back in the 1850s."

"I know what you mean," Alex replied as he looked over. "No telegraph lines, TV aerials, satellite dishes nothing, imagine the life we would have had back then, just you and me out in the wilds, perfect just perfect."

She smiled at him and told him "Come on let's continue over to the old church, see if outcrops up."

They cut across the grass and made their way over to the church wall. They couldn't be bothered with walking around to the entrance so they slipped over the old stone wall while no one was watching.

For some reason, the tourists all kept away from the old church instead they walked around the grave, old cottage and riverside, so it was safe for them both to have a good snoop around the churchyard. The door of the church was open so they entered it but on not finding anything of interest they left it and walked around the graveyard, where they found a familiar name on one of the older gravestones.

JEREMIAH FARTHINGAY

16 JANUARY 1812–12 SEPTEMBER 1864

MOST MISSED HUSBAND OF

MARY

AND FATHER TO

WILLIAM AND ANNE

"It can't be a coincidence that he died here," Alex told her. "One of the mountains that never got searched and he died in the river next to it."

"But I thought that Gabriel said that he himself searched the hills around here," Julie replied.

"He did," Alex told her. "But he didn't know what he was looking for."

"And we do?"

"Yes, we know that if the cavern is hidden around here then it would be marked by the emblem of the Rocket and Bridge."

Julie looked around at all the hills and mountains that surrounded them "Where the hell do we start?"

Alex looked at her and laughed "How the hell do I know, it could be any one of them, it could even be that one there behind the church."

They looked up at the massive mountain overlooking the church; the middle of it was white cliffs surrounded by forests of green. They decided that they would search that one first, but after they had eaten. They walked out of the churchyard and onto the road that led them back to the village. They had a bite to eat in a little tea shop and then set off for the mountain.

It was arduous finding an actual path that took them through the forest and up the side of the mountain, but eventually, they found their way to the bare cliffs. Alex searched the right-hand side while Julie searched the left.

Each of them look over the cliffs and the surrounding rocks for any sign of the emblem. They searched until nightfall without any luck so they gave up for the night and walked back to the village, where they tried to get a room for the night in a local pub. Everywhere was fully booked but they got told about a place just outside the village called the Cwellyn Arms.

The Cwellyn Arms

The Cwellyn Arms is situated on the A4085 Caernarfon to Beddgelert road four miles from Beddgelert, at the base of Snowdon in the Snowdonia National Park. The Hotel let rooms offering a bed and breakfast.

All rooms have en-suite facilities with a power shower and tea and coffee making facilities. Guest also have the convenience of being able to have their meals in the pub which was voted the best real ale pub in Snowdonia by CAMRA. In the summer, you can soak up the sun in the beer garden where weather permitting there is a nightly barbecue which is held by the Excalibur Waterfall.

"Do you believe that?" Julie told him as she read the brochure about the pub. "The Excalibur Waterfall, now that can't be another coincidence can it, we must definitely be in the right place."

"Well, it sounds perfect for us," Alex replied as he phoned it up to see if they had a vacancy.

Luckily they did so they walked back to their car and drove back down the road they had driven up some hours before. After unpacking their things, they decided to make use of the hot summer night, so they walked back to the village and took an amble by the riverside where they sat down on a bench that overlooked the river. After allowing their eyes to get accustomed to the dark, they began to take in the air.

"Do you know that before I met you, I would never have done this," Julie told him.

"Done what?" Alex asked her.

"This," she replied. "Sat outside in the dark."

"Why?"

"Well, I was kinda in a dark place in my life," she replied. "Thinking that I'd die young like the other females in my family, I'd shut myself away, I only went out in daylight, kept in my flat all night just reading books, miserable books about people dying or falling out of love."

Alex looked at her with a confused look on his face.

"Well, I did say I was in a very dark place," she told him. "The last place I wanted to be was in the dark, I would sleep with the lights on afraid that if I turned them off then something would come for me."

"And I finally did," Alex laughed.

"I'm not joking," she cried as she playfully punched him in his side. "But after meeting you, the fear went away and I could sleep with the lights off."

"Only because you didn't want me to see you naked," he replied.

They both started to laugh and cuddled into each other on the bench. Then Julie heard people talking behind them so she looked around to the dogs' grave, where there were still some tourists looking over it, most of them had small dogs with them.

She remembered reading somewhere that if you brought your dog to the village and walked it over to Gelert's Grave then it would extend your dog's life. The stuff of legends she thought but it didn't stop the tourists from flocking to the grave with their dogs.

Alex smiled as he looked at his wife's face as she stared into the mountain facing them. She seemed to be lost in her own thoughts then suddenly she stood up and cried "Oh my God, that's it, bloody hell it's there."

"What's there?" Alex cried. "What's there?"

"That mountain there," she replied. "That's the one, it's so simple."

"What's so simple?"

"The clue," she replied. "I've figured it out, I know what it means."

"What, what does it mean?" he cried as he pulled out his notebook to show her what they had of the clue.

"Look," she told him as she pointed at the clue.

ABC
RVR
DOG   GR

"ABC we take as Arthur's Burial Chamber," she told him. "RVR we know means River. It was only the DOG and GR we couldn't understand, but now I know, it's so simple, it's here. Look that mountain there is where Arthur was buried, there's the River and there is a Dog's Grave, DOG GR."

"My God, you're right," Alex cried. "We've found it, after all this time we have actually found it."

"Then that means," Julie told him as she pointed over to the mountain. "Somewhere under there is the cavern, all we have to do is search it for the emblem."

"It's a big bugger though," Alex told her. "It'll take some searching."

"Maybe but searching one mountain is gonna be a lot simpler than searching all these buggers."

It was too dark to inspect the mountain so they decided to wait until after breakfast the next day. For now, they would go back to their room and look up the mountain and its railway tunnels to see if the date that they were dug out match up to Concerve's journal. On reaching their room, they found that they didn't have a WI-FI connection so they had to go down to the bar where there was one.

After connecting to the internet, they were disappointed to find out that the tunnels were not completed until 1906 and were not used by rail until 1922.

The railway closed in 1937 with the rails requisitioned for War Department use in 1941. In the late 1990s, the Ffestiniog Railway took ownership of the trackbed to rebuild the Welsh High land Railway. In the autumn of 2000, they closed the trackbed to walkers in order to prepare for the rebuilding of the railway.

"So it's now in working order with steam trains running along with it," Alex told her. "It's a good job that it isn't the right one then, I mean imagine us checking the tunnel out and a bloody big locomotive came chugging at us."

"Go back a bit," Julie told him as she spotted something further up the page.

"Why what have you seen?" he asked.

"Maybe nothing but go back up," she told him.

"There," she cried as he scrolled up the page.

In the nineteenth century, with the coming of the Cambrian Railways, numerous schemes were proposed for the construction of a railway to Beddgelert. Somewhere started and there are several examples of abandoned railway works in the past.

"So," Alex told her. "Some work was done but the tunnels were not completed until 1906, that was after Stephenson and Concerve had done their bit."

"Maybe," Julie replied. "Stephenson had started the tunnel and then had a change of heart and stopped digging to preserve the site; look there's a link to a page on Stephenson, click on it."

Alex clicked onto the Stephenson link and was led to a page about Robert Stephenson's attempt to dig through the Aberglaslyn Pass.

In early 1853, Robert Stephenson's attempt to tunnel through the Aberglaslyn Pass came to an abrupt end as the tunnel capsized killing 15 men. An attempt To rescue them resulted in another devastating cave-in so any further work was cancelled and Stephenson placed a memorial on the wall to the men who gave their lives. The memorial still stands today in the middle of the tunnel.

"That has to be it," Julie told him. "Imagine if you wanted to keep something hidden, the best way to stop people from digging is if there was a chance of finding any bodies."

"You think Stephenson lied about the deaths to keep people from digging there?" Alex replied.

"There's a good chance," Julie told him. "Look there's no mention of any of the names of the dead men, it just says there was a memorial to the men who gave their lives, I'm betting if we find the memorial then there would be a Rocket Emblem on it and if so then we have it."

"I suppose there's logic in what you say," Alex replied. "But what about the steam trains, I don't fancy being in the tunnel when they go through."

"We don't know if they do go through, we only know that they go that way, but just in case they do then we'll go first thing before the first train sets off."

They were so wound up that they knew that were was no way that they would be able to sleep so they decided to have a few more drinks being retiring for the night. Julie came back from the bar with a big smile on her face.

"What's up?" he asked.

"Here," she cried as she threw him a brochure she had picked up from a shelf by the bar. "Have a look at that."

"The Sygun Copper Mine," Alex said as he read the brochure.

"Yes," she replied. "It's a tourists place just up the road, and what was Stephenson building a railway for?"

"To transport Copper from the mines to Porthmadog," Alex told her.

"So Bingo," she replied. "We have the mountain, the river, the dog's grave and now a blooming copper mine in the same stretch of hills, we are in the right place."

"Hopefully, so," Alex told her. "And by this time tomorrow, we will have found the emblem to make sure."

"To Tomorrow," Julie cried as she lifted up her pint glass.

First thing in the morning after breakfast they set off for the village. It was still only 8:00 am so the main road was deserted. They passed the shops on the bend and walked along the path that led them to the fields where they crossed the small bridge and jumped over the stile that allowed them onto the field that led them between the mountain and the River Afon Glaslyn.

They followed the river for a while then turned left to follow the Glaslyn's east bank. They then crossed the restored railway line and then continued alongside it. The path led them by the first tunnel and continued right by the water's edge. So they left the path and walked along the rail through the tunnel.

The first tunnel wasn't very long in fact it was more likely a cut through than a tunnel. They couldn't see any memorial on the wall of that one so they continued to the second. This one was a lot longer than the first but again they had no luck in finding anything etched into the wall so they continued along the line with the rushing river below them until they came to the entrance of the third and longest tunnel.

They realised that if there was a memorial then it would be engraved on the left-hand side as the right-hand side just led to the river. They walked for quite a distance until they reached a curve in the track. The light was fading so they each turned on their torch to get a clearer view of the rock walls of the tunnel and slowly moved along the track.

As the bend hid the daylight, it suddenly became dark, very dark. So dark that they couldn't even see one another, even though they were holding hands. That's when Julie's fear of the dark came rushing back to her.

"I can't go any further," she cried. "I have to go back."

"What do you mean?" Alex replied as he got dragged back down the tunnel into the daylight.

"Bloody hell that was bad," she cried as she leant on the damp walls for support while taking a deep breath.

"What's up, are you alright?" Alex asked her.

"Hang on," she cried as she struggled for breath. "That's eerie, one second its daylight the next it's pitch black, I can't go in there, no way can I go in there."

Alex led her to the comfort of the tunnel entrance and sat her down on a rock by the river.

"You'll be okay here," he told her. "Get your breath back and compose yourself, you'll be alright, I'll go in myself and check, I won't be long."

Julie grabbed his hand and pulled him back towards her and told him.

"The light from God was meant to share
But if there's none the Devil's there
If you find a place where light don't reach
Then do not enter is what they teach
For if the light did endeth here
Then go no further for I do fear
That if you go around that bend
Then surely you will meet your end."

"Is that Milton again?" he asked her as he smiled at her.

"No, Julie Anne Ferns 2011," she replied as she kissed his hand. "Be careful, my love, and watch your step it's slippy in there."

He saluted her goodbye and carried on back into the tunnel making his way to the spot where Julie freaked out. When he reached the bend again the daylight disappeared but he carried on regardless, slowly checking the walls for any sign of any engravings. Eventually, he came across something, he couldn't make out any writing on it but it felt like some kind of plaque.

He scraped away at the edges of it to find out its true size. It seemed to be about 2 feet high to 1 feet across and about an inch thick. He scraped some moss of it and managed to make out some words. MEN WHO. He shouted out to Julie that he had found it as he carried on scraping the moss of it until he could read it all.

THIS IS DEDICATED TO THE 15 MEN WHO
GAVE THEIR LIVES IN THE QUEST
OF KNOWLEDGE
AUGUST 1853

He stood back in awe and stared at the memorial plaque and then a thought came over him and he walked back to it and started to scrape just above it. He stopped scraping as he felt another small etching just above the first. He put his hand over his mouth as he felt around the edge and it formed the shape of a shield. He then joined his other hand to his mouth and cupped his face in his hands and took a couple of deep breaths before continuing scraping the remaining moss away.

"Julie, Julie," he shouted as the emblem hit home. "I've found it, it's here, the Rocket Emblem, it's here, I've found it."

He knew that she hadn't heard him so he turned around and went scampering along the track and his beloved wife outside. As soon as she saw him she knew, she couldn't hear him but she knew, the look on his face said it all. She ran down the track and they embraced one another and kissed. He told her of what he had found and she managed to brave her fears and join him back in the darkness of the tunnel so they could look upon it together.

Tears came to her eyes as she read the words on the memorial and she clutched Alex's hand in hers. They inspected the wall and discovered that a small proportion of it was hollow behind it, not much but about a three-foot square that led down and across from the plaque.

Alex realised that they would need to knock through the wall and for that they would need at least a couple of hammers and chisels. They decided to leave it for the rest of the day and come back when darkness had fallen with some tools and some better lighting.

They managed to get hold of a hammer and a chisel from one of the local shops and in the evening they returned to the tunnel each carrying a much larger torch than before. When they reached the tunnel there were still some tourists about sat on the rocks drinking cans of beer, so they followed the path that took them alongside the tunnel and walked by the edge of the river. The path was pushed right by the water edge and they had to grip the handholds that had been screwed into the rocks to assist passage on a short but difficult section.

The path led them into a picnic area at the other side of the mountain which had a building in it that comprised a small sheltered seating area and some toilets. Alex looked at the map on the notice board to pinpoint their position while Julie made use of the conveniences.

When Julie came out Alex told her that through the woods to their right was a camping park and as it was mid-summer then it must be being used so they would have to keep an eye out for the campers coming up to the tunnel.

As they walked through the gateway that took them up to the entrance to the end of the tunnel, they looked down into the picnic area below them as something caught their eye. They didn't have a clue what it was that they could see in the middle of the grass but they decided to have a closer look. It looked like a small sacrificial stone about 3 feet high by 5 feet round that had been placed in a circle that had been cut in the ground. To the left of it stood the remains of what looked like a small cottage that had been buried by centuries of wild growth.

"That's where they used to offer virgins to the Devil," Alex told her. "at least you'll be safe."

"Cheeky bastard, I'll let you know that I was a good girl before I met you," she laughed. "Seriously though, what the hell was it?"

"I don't know for sure," Alex replied as he jumped up and sat on it. "I suppose nowadays it's used for a picnic table but I can't imagine why anyone would build something like this here."

"It doesn't feel right," Julie told him. "I don't think we should be messing about here, especially now the night was falling."

He jumped off the rock and put his arm around her "I've told you, there's no reason to be scared in the dark, not when I'm with you."

"I know," she replied. "But you're not helping with all this talk about Devil worshipping."

"That was only a joke," he told her. "And anyway even if it's true, it was centuries ago, but if you want to go."

"I do," she replied. "Besides we have work to do."

Alex smiled at her as they made their way back up the hill and towards the tunnel entrance "Are you sure that you are okay with this," he asked her. "It's gonna be dark in there, very dark."

"I'll be alright," she told him as she grasped his hand in hers. "But for God's sake, don't let go until we reach the mark."

As soon as they stepped into the tunnel, they felt a chill going through their bodies. It was a lot different at night than going through it in the daytime. In the daytime, you had a bit of light but now they had none but the light from their torches. Every breath they took echoed through the tunnel, every word they spoke came back to them.

It was an eerie feeling walking through in total darkness. They could sense things watching them, it was like the rock-carved walls had eyes of their own and Julie didn't like it. She put her arm around Alex's waist and held on as tight as she could.

"Alex," she cried as she heard a noise a bit further up the track. "What's that?"

"It's nothing, just the sound of us treading on the track echoing back," he told her.

"That's not us walking, there's something in here with us"

"That's just your imagination, relax," he told her. He tried his best to convince her that there was nothing else in there with them but he himself could hear the sound of something else, something not human.

"There," she cried as her torch reflected back off something on the track moving slowly towards them. She screamed as she saw two eyes looking up at her.

"Calm down," Alex told her as he shone his torch onto it. "It's a badger, blow me, it's a bloody badger."

"I told you we were not alone."

"It's okay," Alex replied as the light from the torch sent the badger running off down the tunnel. "It's more scared of us than we are of it."

"How much further is it?" she asked as it seemed they had been treading track for miles.

"It's on the bend," Alex told her. "But in this light, it all seemed to be the same, we could have passed it for all I know."

"You could have left a mark or something," Julie replied.

"Well, I didn't think did I "Alex growled at her. "I didn't realise that it would be like this, it didn't help coming in through the wrong end."

"What's that ahead?" Julie cried as the tunnel started to turn a dark shade of blue.

"It's the bloody moonlight," Alex told her. "We've reached the end of the tunnel."

"You mean we've walked past it."

"We must have, but at least I know my way to it from this way."

As they walked out of the tunnel, they let their eyes get accustomed to the moonlight and then looked to see if the tourists had gone, which they had. Alex asked Julie if she would be alright going back through it. She told him only if he was sure that he could find it this time. He smiled at her and told her to trust him.

Julie took a deep breath and then followed her husband back into the tunnel. This time they did it differently, Julie kept her light on the track while Alex held his against the wall so that they wouldn't miss the memorial again. This time they managed to find it so while Alex started to chip away at the wall Julie kept both lights on where he was working.

"Shit," Alex cried as he heard the echo of the noise he was making. "I'm making quite a din and the tunnel seemed to be making it sound louder than it was, we need to know if we can be heard from outside and if so then how loud was it."

"I take it, it's me who has to go and check," Julie replied.

"Either that or you stay here and hammer away while I go to check the noise outside."

"Bugger that," Julie told him. "I'm not stopping here by myself, I'll go and check the noise if it's not noticeable I'll be back in a bit but if it's loud then I'll stay outside and keep watch."

"Are you sure that you'll be alright?" Alex asked her.

"We don't have much of a choice do we," she replied as she walked down the tunnel.

Ten minutes later she returned to tell him that you could hear the banging faintly but there was no way that she was staying out there by herself, so they would have to take the chance that they wouldn't be disturbed.

"I'm almost through," he told her. "Yes, that's it," he cried as he pulled a brick. "The top is all rock but up to my neck is mainly brick, some of it has rock behind but this piece has nothing behind it, my hand goes right through and I can feel a draught behind it."

"Here let me shine the torch up to you," Julie told him as he carried on hitting the next brick.

"These are coming away a lot easier," he told her as he quickly removed brick after brick until he had a hole big enough to look through. "Here pass me a torch."

She passed him a torch and he peered through the small hole, moving the light from the torch slowly around the dark cavern behind. "Can you see out?" Julie asked.

"Nothing yet," he told her. "Hang on a tick, there's something there."

"What is it?" Julie asked excitedly.

"Can't make it out," he replied as he shoved his face closer into the hole. "It looks like a statue, ah hang on I can make it out now. It's a tall cross, about 8 feet tall."

"Arthur's," she asked.

"Can't tell, it's too far away."

"Can you see out else?" she asked him as she tried herself to peer through the hole.

"Yes," he cried as he moved away to let her see. "I could see what looked like a large stone box behind the cross, can you see it?"

"No," she told him as she squinted her eyes. "I can see the cross but not the box."

"Have you brought your glasses with you?" he asked her as he laughed.

"Cheeky get," she cried as she pulled her head out of the hole. "I don't need them now, contact lenses remember."

"I'm only joking, the box is to the left of the cross just behind it," he told her as he looked through the hole. "I think we need to remove some more bricks so that we can enter the cavern."

They remove more bricks, not a lot but just enough for them to be able to pass through the wall and enter the cavern. As Alex tried to get into the cavern, he knocked a brick and it fell down. That's then he realised that there was a small drop into it.

He shone his torch down to see how far the drop was. It was only about 3 feet, but it still would have caused injury to him if he had just walked into it. It was a good job then that he had dropped the brick into it.

A highly excitable Alex went first followed by a more nervous Julie. Alex helped her down into the cavern. It wasn't a cavern it was a small room made from brick, man-made about 150 years old. Even the roof was made from brick; it didn't make sense why would anyone go to the trouble of building a room underneath a mountain and then seal it up. They shone their torches around for a while and then they both looked over to the cross.

"Is it Arthur's?" she asked.

"No," he replied as he shone his light onto it. "There's an engraving on it, it says

"IN MEMORY OF
THOSE WHO DIED
IN DIGGING OUT
THIS TUNNEL
16 AUGUST 1853"

"Look," she cried as she spotted some names running along the side of the cross. "The memorial was real, people really did die here."

"15," Alex told her as he counted the dead men's names that circled the middle of the cross. "Hang on a tick, what's this?"

"What's what?" she asked.

"Bloody hell, it's a sword," he cried.

"Where."

"On the top of the cross running down it, can you see it," he told her as he shone his light on it to show an etching of a large sword that seemed to have been placed perfectly into the cross so that the handles of the sword were directly in the centre of the cross itself.

"I take it that was supposed to be Excalibur?" Julie asked.

"Can't be anything else," Alex told her as he moved over to the stone box. "Looks like a stone well with a slab covering it," he shouted to Julie who was still marvelling at the sword on the cross.

"I've seen these in old graveyards," Julie told him. "If I'm not mistaken they lead down to crypts where bodies are kept."

"Arthur," they both cried in unison.

"If it's Arthur's, then there must be a name or something on it," Julie told him as she scanned the top of the slab with her torch. "There's something but I can't make it out," she told him.

"IN MEMORY

OF

JOHN BRONES

A GOOD FRIEND

AND SCHOLAR

DIED 17 MAY 1852"

"John Brones?" Alex said. "Wasn't he the guy who the cavern collapsed on when Concerve was here?"

"Yes," Julie told him. "He was the one who spoke Latin, he read out Arthur's cross to them."

"The Scholar," Alex cried. "So it's true then it's all true."

"So if Brones existed," Julie told him excitedly. "Then so must Arthur's cavern."

They both looked around the room but couldn't see any other entry or blocked up doorways, there was only one place where the cavern could be. They both looked back to Brone's Grave.

"It has to be under there," Alex told her. "Didn't you say that these things had crypts under them?"

"As far as I know, they do," Julie replied.

"Come on then," he cried. "Give me a hand; see if we can move this thing."

Julie walked over to him and they both tried with all their might to push the slab off but without success. "We need a big bar or something," Alex told her. "To prise the bugger off."

"We can't leave it like this," Julie told him. "We are here, we are stones thrown from the greatest discovery ever, we can't give up now."

"We are not giving up," Alex told her. "But we need more light and we need more manpower, especially to move that bugger."

"You mean Gabriel," Julie asked.

"Yes, he's the only one we can trust."

"But he's in hospital; he's had a heart attack."

"Yes, but he's getting better and he deserves to be here when we open it, plus he's a big bugger and we need him."

"I thought you said that he had given up."

"He had but this may be just what he needs to get the strength to carry on."

"Are you sure that we can trust him?"

"We've no choice, my love; we can't exactly call the AA can we."

"But what about this place, we can't leave it open, what if anyone comes along."

"What at this time of night with a torch and a crowbar what's the chance of that?"

"There have been too many coincidences already on this quest, besides you know our luck."

"All we can do is once we are back out in the tunnel is to replace the bricks; hopefully, no one will notice."

"I'll be happier knowing that the hole was covered," Julie told him as she headed to the hole in the wall.

Alex helped her up and once she was out she gave her hand to him to help pull him out. They then replaced most of the bricks and once they were satisfied that no one would notice the brick room they set off back to their hotel.

On reaching the Cwellyn Arms, they had a shower before retiring for the night. They both didn't get a wink of sleep as they were still hyped up about their discovery. They spent the rest of the night just lying on the bed talking to each other until dawn broke, and after breakfast, they went to visit Gabriel in Aberystwyth.

It took them a couple of hours to drive to the hospital and when they arrived they were surprised to find Gabriel sat up in his bed looking like there was nothing wrong with him. As soon as they entered the room, the look on their faces told him everything.

"You found it!" he cried as he jumped up from the bed. Julie nodded. "I knew you'd find it. You make a damn fine pair you know that."

"Don't count your chicken's yet," Alex told him as Gabriel put his hands on his shoulders as if to hug him.

"But you said you found it?"

"We found something," Alex told him.

"A brick room built inside a mountain," Julie cried as she interrupted Alex.

"With a memorial cross and a burial slab with John Brones name on it," Alex told him.

"Brones, John Brones," Gabriel cried. "You've found his grave?"

"We're not sure," Alex replied. "We've found what we think is a crypt in a hidden room built within a railway tunnel under a mountain in Beddgelert."

"Beddgelert eh, I've bloody searched there," Gabriel told him.

"The name on the crypt is John Brones," Alex told him as he carried on. "And the year inscribed on it was 1852."

"1852?" Gabriel replied. "That was the year of their expedition."

"We think," Julie told him. "That the crypt will lead us down to Arthur's Cavern."

"But we couldn't get the top off the crypt," Alex said as he interrupted her.

"So you need some help do you?" Gabriel asked.

"Yes," Julie replied. "He's not as strong as he thought he was."

"It's a very heavy slab," Alex told him as Julie poked her tongue out at him.

"So you came to me for help," Gabriel asked.

"Only if you're up to it?" Julie asked.

"Even if I'd lost both my legs I'd still say yes," Gabriel replied as he grabbed Alex's shoulders and shook them "Come on lad, let's be going."

"We'll have to hurry we left it half-open," Julie told him.

"You left it open?" Gabriel cried. "The gateway to the greatest historical discovery of our time and you left it open?"

"Well, we have bricked it back up," Julie replied. "But if anyone leant against it, there's a chance that they'd dislodged it."

"But the chance of that is absolutely nil," Alex snapped. "The place where it was would only be discovered if you were looking for it. It's pitch black in there so anyone walking through will walk along the track in the centre."

"The track?" Gabriel asked. "There's still a damn track in there?"

"Still trains going through it," Julie replied.

"Trains!"

"Not big trains," Alex told him. "Steam locomotives, the Welsh Highland Railway has rebuilt the full line, from Porthmadog to Caernarfon, it runs right around and through parts of the mountains."

"You're joking," Gabriel replied as he smiled at Julie. "You're telling me that after all this time over 150 years since they set out to build the railway, my ancestors' railway line was complete, I can't believe, I knew that there were men working on the tunnels when I last checked the area over two years ago but I never for the life of me thought that they were rebuilding the whole line."

"You live and learn," Alex told him. "Now come on we have a bit of shopping to do."

"Shopping?"

"Yes," Alex told him. "We need more light than what we have, I've seen lightweight portable generators advertised so I'm gonna pick one up and light up the full cavern, if it's there then I want to see it, all of it."

On the way back to Beddgelert, they managed to find a warehouse that specialised in building equipment so they picked up a small petrol generator and three retractable spot lamps on stands. They just managed to fit the generator in the car boot, the lights found a place across the back seat next to Gabriel.

It took them another hour to get to the village where they treated Gabriel to lunch at Lyn's Tea Shop, a small place just down a side road from the shops. After lunch, they had a walk along the river bank and they showed him the mountain and they watched as a steam train passed through the first set of tunnels.

Gabriel smiled as he looked over at the mountain "I never bothered with that one," he told them. "I thought that if there had been a railway through the mountain then to ignore it, I thought Stephenson wouldn't have tunnelled through the mountain in case he disturbed the cavern."

"He didn't," Julie replied. "He only dug so far and we think that he faked a cave-in to protect the cavern from being discovered, he left a memorial to the men who died, but we think it was a cover-up to stop people from digging there."

"Yes," Gabriel cried. "He was a clever man, what better way to stop men from digging, I mean who would dig if there was a chance of disturbing the dead."

"Exactly," Alex told him. "The tunnel was completed in the early 1900s, way after your ancestor had searched, he would have been around while Stephenson was digging it out in 1853, what better way to get rid of a snoop than working on the one mountain that he shouldn't have been anywhere near, I mean who would think of hiding something so close to where everyone passed, that's where Stephenson and Concerve were clever, Stephenson was the designer, he most probably stayed behind and designed the room, whoever worked on it would have thought that they were building a memorial and not known that they were building a cover to stop the cavern from ever being discovered."

Julie looked over the river towards the mountain "It's gonna be a bugger getting all the equipment to the tunnel," she told them. "It was very hard going just for us to walk there."

"I've been thinking about that," Alex replied. "We're not going that way, remember the second time we went to the tunnel, we went around the other side and got in that way. There is a small car park next to the toilet building you used, if we can find the road that led to it then it was only about five minutes to the entry of the tunnel."

Julie poked her tongue out at him and called him a smart arse while he pulled out a map from his jacket pocket. It was quite easy to find the lane that led to the car park in the daytime but it would be harder at night, so they took note of the red bin that was dumped in the bushes just before it. If they found the bin then they would know that the lane was coming up.

Chapter Nine
The Tomb

King Arthur's
Burial Cross

As darkness approached, they set off for the car park next to the toilet. They parked the car and unloaded the lamps and generator from the car boot. Luckily the generator had a built on a trolley so Julie pulled that while Alex carried the three spot lamps and Gabriel carried a small crowbar, a large crowbar and the torches. As they walked up the path that led them to the tunnel, they heard a noise coming from the picnic site below them.

They looked down to see a courting couple making out on the round stone that Alex said was where they sacrificed virgins.

"Told you it was where they sacrificed virgins," he whispered to Julie.

"She doesn't look like a virgin to me," Julie replied.

"It's a fertility stone," Gabriel told them. "Legend has it if you make love on the stone it improves your chances of conceiving."

"Does it work?" Julie asked.

"Couldn't tell you," Gabriel replied. "But I can tell you that loads of childless couples have tried it."

Julie smiled and looked over to Alex "Don't even think about it," Alex told her. "I'm not the fathering kind."

"Will you two be quiet," Gabriel whispered. "We've got work to do."

Julie stuck her tongue out at Alex as they continued up to the tunnel's entrance.

Unlike the last time they entered the tunnel this way, this time they found the bricked up room straight away. Seeing as the bricks were loose they quickly removed them and Alex jumped down into the room. Gabriel dropped him the lamps, the generator and the crowbars and then entered himself quickly followed by Julie.

While Alex was fiddling about trying to start the generator Julie showed Gabriel the cross and then Brones' tomb.

"After all this time, I've finally found you," Gabriel cried as he rubbed his hand along Brones memorial slab. "It looks heavy this," he shouted to Alex. "Are you sure we can get it open?"

"The three of us might," Julie replied as she heard the generator come spluttering to life.

"Now we have light," Alex cried as he connected the first spot lamp to the generator. "Now let's see what we have here," he shouted as he connected the second lamp.

Now it was brighter than a day in the old long-forgotten room. To Julie's disappointment, there was nothing else of interest in the room, all the light did was to allow them a better view of what they had already seen. The only other object in the room was a small wooden box containing some old bottles.

"Do you fancy a drink," Julie laughed as she pulled out a black onion shaped bottle with Dewars Perth Whisky engraved on the front. "It hasn't even been opened."

"They must have been celebrating something though," Gabriel cried as he pulled out about nine empty green beer bottles. "Here's another full one, Dr Soules, Hop Bitter."

"That will taste bitter if you drank it," Alex replied as he also looked into the box. "What are those at the bottom?"

"I don't know," Gabriel told him as he pulled out a couple of small green ball-shaped bottles that still had their contents in. "Harding's Fire Grenade."

"A fire grenade," Julie cried. "What's a bloody fire grenade?"

"Hey, I've heard about those," Alex told her as he pulled one out of the box. "We had some on display as far as I can remember the bottle contained a liquid, what was it now? I remember, it contained Carbon Tetrachloride and what they did was throw it into a fire and when the bottle broke it helped to douse the flames."

"Listen to Mr Cleverclogs here," Julie laughed.

"They must have brought them down here in case they caused a fire while digging it out," he told her as he picked two up and put them into his pocket.

"Shit!" he cried as he went back to the task of removing the slab.

"What's up?" Gabriel asked.

"I've cocked up," he replied. "Even if we get the slab off the tomb, the generator is too big to fit inside it."

"That's a damn bugger," Gabriel replied. "Anything we can do about it."

"We need an extension cable," Julie told them. "If we get an extension we could run a wire from here down to whatever was down there."

"Good idea," Gabriel replied. "But where can we get a cable from?"

"What time is it?" Alex asked.

"8:30," Julie told him. "Why?"

"If I could find a petrol station," Alex replied. "Then maybe I could buy one or two."

"The only garage around here was about 10 miles back on the A4085 towards Llanfrothen," Gabriel told him. "I think it's only open while 10."

"That'll have to do," Alex replied. "Does it have a good stock?"

"It's got a shop, but I don't know what it sold."

"We've no choice," Alex told him. "If we go down there, we're gonna need a lot of light, are you two gonna be alright in here?"

"As long as you're quick," Julie told him as she kissed him goodbye. "And don't waste time ogling those lovers out there."

Alex smiled as he set off down the tunnel and back towards his car. Luckily the garage was open and it did stock extension cables. He bought three just to be on the safe side and he was back in the tunnel within the hour.

Alex set to work with the small crowbar trying to get it between the slab and the top of the tomb. Eventually, he got it in, and with Gabriel's help, they managed to raise it just enough to enable Julie to insert the larger crowbar in the gap that they had made.

Once the big crowbar was in place, they lowered the slab back down and removed the smaller one. Between them, Alex and Gabriel pushed down onto the large crowbar, and after a bit of a struggle, they managed to slide it a bit. Not much but just enough for them to be able to shine a torch down and take a look. Gabriel smiled at Alex as instead of seeing a pile of bones they saw a flight of stone steps that took them further underground.

They realised straight away that the tomb wasn't a tomb it was as they had hoped the gateway to another passageway. Hopefully, this one led them to the place they had been searching for King Arthur's Burial Chamber.

By using both crowbars, they managed to prise the tomb open enough for them to enter it. They were careful not to tip the slab off completely because they knew that afterwards, they would have to reseal it and if the slab fell then it would be impossible to lift it back up.

Gabriel was first down, followed by Julie who was helped down by Alex who then followed himself. There was no point in taking the spot lamps yet just in case there was nothing down there. So they just took their torches and slowly made their way along the passage.

After about 40 yards, they came across a dead end. At first, it puzzled them but then they realised that Stephenson being a very clever man would have been able to work out exactly how far the cavern was from where he had tunnelled, so it wouldn't have been too much for him to have been able to stop digging just before they hit the cavern wall.

Alex decided to break through so he went back to the tomb to retrieve the large crowbar. "Here goes," he shouted as he started to jab the crowbar into the wall. At first, nothing, it was just lumps of clay falling down but suddenly the crowbar went straight through the wall and Alex could feel nothing at all behind it. He smiled at the Lord and then started to attack the wall from all angles until he had broken a gap through big enough for them to get through.

It didn't lead them into King Arthur's Cavern though; it was just the entrance into another passageway. So one by one they followed it. They didn't have a clue which way it was leading them, in the darkness of the tunnel they couldn't tell whether they were heading left or right. Alex kept walking into the wooden

149

supports that were scattered throughout the passageway. Gabriel warned him to be careful otherwise he could cause a cave-in.

Then suddenly they happened across something that had Alex very excited. It was a damp wall covered in moss. He remembered the journal and that the entrance was behind a wall of moss so he eagerly edged ahead of Gabriel and led the way forward himself. In the distance, he could see a glare ahead of him. He thought he was seeing things, how could there be a bright light there? This far underground. It didn't seem possible.

His heart was beating as he reached the glare. But he was disappointed to find it to be another dead end with no sign of light there. What the hell was going on? He could swear that he had seen a light ahead of him. Gabriel and Julie didn't see it themselves and just thought that it was Alex's mind playing tricks on him.

"There was something," Alex shouted. "A tiny glare, it was coming from here."

"But there's nowt here," Julie told him. "Just another dead end."

"He may not be as mad as we think," Gabriel cried. "Look at this wall, it's not clay, it's like stone."

"Could be a door," Alex told him. "Remember in Egyptian times when they were making the tombs for the Kings they always cut another way out just in case of cave-ins, maybe who ever built Arthur's chamber built a second entrance."

"You could be right," Julie replied. "See if there are any edges."

Gabriel checked around the stone wall while Alex lit it up with his torch "There," Gabriel cried as he ran his fingers along a line in the stone. He followed it around blowing the dust from it and it showed the outline of a doorway. "How do we get it open?"

"Forget about nice-a-tices," Alex cried as he stabbed the crowbar into the lines around the door and started to scrape along with it. Once he had a good hold in the stonework, he began to break away the rocky surface. After a good half an hour, he got the first stone loose, and with a mighty heave, he managed to shove it through into whatever lay behind it. After that, it was quite easy removing the stone and once they had got a few out they shone a torch through to have a look at what was behind the wall.

At first, he couldn't see anything but as he shone the torch around he caught glimpse of something on the floor facing him. It reflected the light when he shone it down. He couldn't tell what it was, but he knew that it was definitely metal of sorts. He then handed the torch back to Julie while he removed stone after stone, until finally, they could climb through it.

As they all entered the room and allowed their eyes to get accustomed to the dark, they shone their torches around to see what was in this cavern that they had discovered. They discovered the bodies of 15 men in armour, ancient armour, but strangely the suits were empty, the bodies had long since turned to dust. Their torches were not powerful enough to inspect the cavern as close as they wanted so while Gabriel and Julie looked around Alex went back to the tomb to bring down and set up the spot lamps.

Within 20 minutes, they had the cavern lit up as bright as day and the first thing to hit them was the way the light reflected off the far wall.

"Golden walls," Gabriel cried. "I thought it was a myth but look it's true, the walls are golden."

"That's not gold," Alex told him as he took a scraping. "It's Iron Pyrite."

"Iron pirates," Gabriel asked. "What the hell is iron pirates? It looks like gold to me."

"It's commonly known as Fools Gold, you must have heard of that?" Alex told him.

"How do you know?" Julie asked. "It does look like gold."

"It's just a mineral, it's fooled people for generations, I only know about it because someone brought some into the Museum I used to work in but I didn't think that you could find a full wall of it, I thought you found it in clusters."

Iron Pyrite is an iron sulphide with the formula FeS_2
This mineral's metallic lustre and pale-to-normal
Brass-yellow hue have earned it the nickname of
Fool's Gold because of its resemblance to Gold.
Pyrite is usually found with other sulphides, oxides
In quartz veins, sedimentary rock and metamorphic
Rock as well as in coal beds.

"So it's not worth out then?" Julie asked.

"All minerals are worth something," Alex replied. "Just nowhere near the price of gold."

"Well, at least this is all gold," Gabriel told him as he waded through the two piles of silver, gold and jewelled oddments in the middle of the floor.

Alex wasn't interested in the treasures he and Julie were more interested in which knight was King Arthur. They both decided that it was the one that was laid separately from the rest so they walked over to him. By his side lay a still sparkling sword and a jewelled shield.

"This was Arthur," Alex cried.

"Are you sure?" Julie asked.

"Yes," Alex replied. "Look at the shield and the sword they both have the same symbol as the one on the knight's armour. And it's Arthur's mark, the sign of the virgin and the black crow."

"Are you sure it's his mark?" Julie asked. "What does it mean?"

"Didn't you read Concerve's Journal?" Alex asked her.

"I skipped through it," she replied. "I can't remember everything," she told him as he gave her a disappointed look.

"The virgin was the badge of the ideal Christian leader against the Pagan foe and the crow was what Arthur was supposed to be re-incarnated as."

"Hey, look at this," Gabriel cried as he held up a solid gold face mask. "Do you think this was Arthur's?"

"No," Julie replied. "It's too small; it looked like a child's mask."

"Hey, Alex," Julie replied. "Look over there, there's a small cross."

"That was mentioned in the journal," He shouted as he got to his feet and joined her.

"HIC IACET SEPULTUS INCLYTUS REX ARTURIES," Julie said as she tried to read it. "I think that's right, I never did take Latin at school."

"According to Concerve, it means. The great King Arthur is buried here."

"Well, you can keep your history," Gabriel shouted. "I'll keep the riches, there's all sorts here, diamonds, rubies, pearls, and gold bracelets, even a pair of golden gloves encased with silver beading."

"I thought you weren't interested in money," Julie snapped. "I thought you were only after the glory of finding it."

"We all deserve to treat ourselves from time to time and I'm treating myself to a new pair of gloves."

"He's got a point," Alex told her. "Have a look, see if anything catches your fancy."

"I suppose something small won't bother me," Julie replied as she knelt down by the piles of oddments.

As they stared at the marvel of the cavern and started to sort through the jewels, gems and golden artefacts on the floor, the cavern got plunged back into darkness as the generator cut out.

"What's happened?" Julie screamed.

"It's okay," Alex replied. "Generators cut out that's all, switch on your torches while I go back up and sort it out."

As they turned on their torches, Alex wandered up the tunnel to get back to the crypt "What the hell?" he cried as he reached the bottom of the steps to see that the slab had been replaced. "How the heck did that fallback?" He tried to push the slab up but it wouldn't budge so he shouted to the others to join him.

"You're joking," Julie cried as he told her what had happened. "It couldn't have moved by itself it took all three of us to move it."

"Well, it's got back somehow," Gabriel replied. "Maybe this place be cursed after all."

"It wasn't some kind of magic that moved it," Alex told him. "There must be someone else up there, look the cable has been disconnected not cut through by the weight of the slab falling on it."

"But who?" asked Julie. "No one else knows, or do they," she said as she turned her torch into Gabriel's face.

"Don't look at me," he told her. "Only me and the lad knew, no one else."

"Could he have told anyone?" Alex asked.

"He wasn't like that."

"Oh," Julie cried. "He was a murdering scumbag but he wouldn't double-cross you."

"He had no need girl; he got whatever he wanted of me."

"Well, someone's up there," Alex told him as he started to shout for help.

"No one's listening, lad," Gabriel told him. "But we know something that they don't."

"What's that?"

"There is another entrance remember, the original passage, the one that poor Brones got buried in."

"But it caved in, we can't get out that way," Julie cried.

"It's our only chance," Gabriel told them.

"If it exists," Alex replied.

"Oh it exists alright; it must do, after all, everything else in your journal does, if we can find it, maybe we can remove the fallen debris and force our way out."

"How," Julie asked. "We haven't any spades, how can we dig our way out through the original passage."

"We'll use our crowbars to dig," Alex told her.

"And our hands to scrape the fallen rocks away," Gabriel replied.

"Well, we best be quick," Julie told them. "For our torches won't last much longer using them all the time. And I don't want to be down here in the pitch dark."

"Don't worry, my love," Alex told her as he gave her a cuddle. "We've been in worse places than this."

They quickly discovered where the original passageway was and started moving the fallen debris out of what was remaining of the opening. They were making good progress, rock after rock and handfuls of earth were quickly dispatched from the passageway.

Alex had the bright idea of using the chest plates from the suits of armour as shovels and they easily dug their way through. Suddenly they heard a clang as their homemade shovel struck something metal.

"What is it?" Julie asked as Gabriel worked furiously with his hands to chicken scratch around the object.

"Oh my God!" he cried as he saw the glimpse of gold shining through the earth. "It's the bell; it's the bell of Mordred."

"Don't touch it," Julie cried. "It's cursed, everyone who has ever touched it has either died or gone blind."

"It's in our way love," Gabriel replied. "It has to come out."

"Be careful," Alex cried. "Here let me scrape it out with this chest plate."

"You'd never move it laddie, it's solid gold," Gabriel told him as he shoved his hands through the earth and grabbed the bell from behind. "It's moving," he cried as he slowly managed to pull it out.

"What's that on it?" Julie shouted as something came out with the bell. "It looks like an arm."

"Bugger me," Gabriel cried as he shone his light upon it. "It is, it's a bloody hand."

"We've found Brones," Alex cried as he moved some more rocks from the passageway. "Or what remained of him."

"Just rags and bones," Gabriel shouted as he removed all the debris off the remains of John Brones. "Strange it doesn't smell, you would have thought it'll stink by now."

"It's only dead bodies that smell," Alex told him. "And that hasn't been a body for many a year."

They removed the remains and placed them by the armour of Arthur. They had a feeling that he would have wanted to be laid to rest by the king. As Julie and Alex continued to dig their way out, Gabriel wasn't with them; he was too busy examining the bell.

"Gabriel, come on," Julie shouted. "We haven't got time."

"I'll be there in a sec," Gabriel replied. "I'm just checking something."

They couldn't leave him so they went back into the cavern where they saw him dusting down the golden bell. As he saw them return, he looked up at them both and told them that the bell had an etching on it.

"It's a warning," Alex shouted.

"How do you know?" Gabriel cried.

Julie and Alex told him that it was mentioned in Concerve's journal.

"You shouldn't touch it," Julie cried. "We told you not to touch it."

"You don't believe in all that mumbo jumbo do you?" Gabriel replied as he spat on the bell to clean the dried earth from it. "We have to take it with us."

"Don't be so foolish," Alex shouted. "It's too heavy."

"And it's not worth the risk," Julie added. "It's gonna be hard enough for us to get out of here."

"And I'm not wasting much-needed oxygen carrying that thing," Alex told him.

"You two don't have to do anything I'll take it," Gabriel told them as he got to his feet and started to drag the bell.

"Gabriel," Alex shouted. "It's not worth it, the strain of carrying that, think what it'll do to your heart."

"Beggar me heart," Gabriel shouted back as he bent down to try to pick it up. "Actually, I think I'd be able to carry it."

"Gabriel doesn't attempt to…" Alex couldn't finish for as he tried to warn Gabriel about lifting it up; he collapsed to the floor holding his arm. "Julie, come quick," Alex shouted as he raced to Gabriel's side.

"What is it?" she cried as she saw Alex by Gabriel's side.

"I think he's having a heart attack," Alex shouted.

With neither of them being medically trained, they didn't have a clue on how to help someone who was having a heart attack. They tried everything they knew but nothing was helping. It was as if Gabriel had wanted this. To die, here, in the cavern of Arthur. The place he had spent his life searching for. He kept pushing them away as they tried desperately to keep him alive.

"You can't die," Alex cried as he and Julie knelt beside the dying Lord. "You have so much to live for."

Gabriel looked up to him and grabbed his hand, and with his dying breath, he placed Alex's hand into his open jacket and pointed to the pocket and then he died.

"He's gone," a deeply upset Alex told a weeping Julie as he reached into Gabriel's pocket and pulled out an envelope, which was strangely addressed to him.

"What is it?" Julie asked as she saw the envelope.

"A letter," Alex replied as he wiped his eyes. "Addressed to me."

"To you," Julie cried. "What the hell did he write to you about?"

"It's not the time now," Alex told her as he slipped the letter into his pocket. "We better lay him to rest, we'll place him by the side of Arthur with Brones, it's what he would have wanted."

They dragged him to Arthur's side and placed the bell of Mordred by his side using the chest plate to push it into place rather than touch it themselves. After saying a short prayer, they went back to the task of getting out of the tunnel.

On clearing some more rocks out of the way, they could see a clear passageway ahead of them. They scrambled through the debris and once over they could actually stand up. They dusted themselves down and followed the passageway until they reached another pile of rocks.

"This must be where Stephenson and Concerve caved in the entrance before they left for Porthmadog," Alex told her as he set about removing the first few rocks out of the way. "It can't be that far now until we reach the hillside."

They each took it in turns to have a go at removing the debris from in front of them. They had to be careful removing the bigger rocks in case they started another landslide. Finally, they removed the last of the large rocks and all that lay before them now seemed to be earth and clay. He needed something to jab his way through so he went back to the cavern to pick up one of the large crowbars. When he returned he started to jab the crowbar into the earth and twist it. He soon worked up a rhythm and began to jab and jab, until finally, he broke through.

"I can see daylight," Alex cried as the crowbar broke through the side of the hill. He gripped the wet earth from outside and started to rip and push his way through until he could fit his head through the hole. He took a deep breath of much-needed fresh air and then allowed Julie to do the same before he continued to force his way out.

Eventually, they both got out and they found themselves on the small steep path that ran between the hill and the river. After taking a short rest, they got up and made their way back to the tunnel entrance to see what the hell had happened in the bricked-up room.

As they reached the picnic spot, they saw an orange light coming from the car park. Their car was on fire. They ran to it, but it was too late to save it. Alex stood on the hill watching his new car going up in flames. He looked at Julie and threw his hands up in the air.

"This can't be happening," he cried. "Who the heck could do this, what the hell do they want?"

Julie shrugged her shoulders as she couldn't answer him.

"Hang on a tick," he told her as he searched his pockets. "I've got those fire grenades here."

"You're not expecting them to work?" Julie replied as Alex tossed them into the burning car.

"That was a waste of time," he cried as nothing happened except the sound of breaking glass.

"I don't believe you," Julie told him. "They're over a hundred years old."

"They were still unused though," he replied. "They should have done more than just go plop."

"Times change you dimwit," Julie told him. "In the day, they were used they never had cars full of petrol."

"Okay," he replied. "So I'm thick but I'm still puzzled about what the hell was going on."

Alex knew that the only answer would come from the tunnel so he set off back up the hill to the entrance. Julie tried to hold him back. What if they're still there? But Alex wanted answers and he wanted them now. There was still some power left in the only torch that they had managed to save so they wearily made their way into the tunnel.

To save the batteries and also to protect themselves Alex turned off the light and grabbed her hands. He told her not to worry and keep a tight grip as they walked slowly along the track. He told her to let her eyes get accustomed to the dark and that they needed to do this way so has not be seen. They gradually got further and further into the tunnel, Alex fell to the ground twice by slipping on the wet track.

Suddenly he turned the light on as he couldn't see any sign of light up ahead. "Whoever was here," he whispered. "They must have already gone because there was no torchlight ahead." He lit up the side of the tunnel and realised that they had gone past the tomb so they turned around and went back. When they reached the tomb they couldn't believe their eyes, for it had been bricked up.

"What the hell is going on?" Julie asked him. "How could they have done this in such a short time?"

"Must have been quite a few of them," Alex told her. "Not only had they put the bricks back but they have cemented them as well."

"Are we in the right place?"

"Yes, look the cement's still wet, and up there is the emblem."

"I think we best get out of here," Julie replied. "There are forces at work here that I can't comprehend."

Alex agreed with her and he grabbed her hand again and started off down the tunnel.

As they reached the end of the tunnel, they were met by four men, two of which were holding hunting knives.

"I told you they were clever," the smallest one said to the others.

"They can't be that clever," the middle guy replied. "Otherwise they'd be far away from here by now."

"Where's the other one?" a tall guy who introduced himself as Paul asked them. "The older guy, where is he?"

"I know you don't I?" Alex asked the small guy. "You run the hotel where we are staying."

"What if I do?" the small guy replied.

"Forget about him," Paul cried. "Where's the other guy?"

"Back there," Julie replied as she nodded towards the tunnel.

"He's dead," Alex told them. "He had a heart attack while we were digging our way out."

"Who are you?" Julie asked. "What do you want with us?"

"I suppose I must introduce ourselves to you," Paul replied. "I'm Paul, the blonde one's Peter, you know short horse, Johnno, here and he's Owain."

"What do you want of us?" Alex asked.

"It's not what we want," Johnno replied. "It's what we must do, what we have to do."

"You know too much," Peter told them. "You should never have gone into that tomb."

"Yeah," cried Owain. "You sealed your fate when you unsealed the tomb."

"You can't be serious," Julie replied. "You're gonna kill us, do you actually know what's in there?"

"My girl," Paul told her. "Of course we know, we've always known."

"How?" asked Alex. "How could you know?"

"Tell me what you know," Paul replied. "And how you found it, you never know it may save your lives."

"Don't tell him, Alex," Julie cried. "He's just fishing to see if anyone else would be looking for it."

"You are a smart wee thing," Paul replied. "True we can't be having anyone else looking for it, but I am curious about how you did find it."

Alex knew he was beaten, there was no way that they could take on all four, true they were just four average men but two had knives and he wasn't going to get his wife stabbed to death, if they were going to die then they would die together. He told them all he knew and all that they had been through on their quest for King Arthur's Cavern. On hearing their story, the four men looked at one another and Paul explained who they were and why they were doing the things they were.

"History," he cried. "You're here because you followed your ancestor's journal; we're here because we are following our ancestor's wishes."

"What do you mean?" Alex asked as he and Julie got made to sit against the wall of the tunnel.

As they pushed them to the ground, Julie noticed a tattoo on Peter's arm. "Alex," she whispered. "Look at his arm, that tattoo it's the same as the emblem, the Rocket on a Bridge."

"I've seen it," he replied.

"What are you two whispering about?" Paul asked.

"Your tattoo," Alex replied. "It matches the emblem that we have found next to all the clues that we have been following."

"This one," Paul replied as he pointed to his arm. "We all have this one, it's a kind of membership sign."

"Membership sign," Alex asked. "What the hell are you lot members off?"

"We all belong to the Order of the Brotherhood of the Light Beings," Paul told him.

"The Light Beings," Alex asked. "What's that?"

"The Brotherhood of the Light Beings was set up by your ancestor's best mate, Robert Stephenson. He set it up as an order to protect the cavern from ever being discovered. He realised that man was too greedy to share the knowledge about what lay beneath this mountain.

So he entrusted the safety of it to a group of local men who he had befriended. He trusted them with the knowledge and they all agreed that the cavern should never be discovered. So they dug out the room and made sure that the rest of the village heard a story about men dying in a cave in."

"The Light Beings," Julie cried. "Concerve warned us to beware of the Light Being man, beware the greedy man and the Light Being man, I remember now but at the time it went over my head, I read it but I never once thought about who the Light Being man was?"

"We are all descendants of the men who built the tomb," Owain told them as he interrupted Paul. "Men who swore on oath to Stephenson that they'll guard and protect the secret of what lay beneath the mountain."

"The secret of the cavern was passed down from father to son, to son to son and so on," Peter told them as he interrupted Owain. "Our forefathers took a pledge to protect the mountain and we have done since."

"Until the time was right," Paul cried. "Until the people are ready to cope with the knowledge that was down there."

"People will never be ready," Owain told them. "The politicians and the like of today could not be trusted with the secret; they are only in it for what they can get out of it.

"Power is all they are after and how they can use it to better themselves. You think that they'll share it between the people of Wales like Stephenson wanted, no my friend they'll keep it hidden and share the treasure between each other, and we are here to make sure that that doesn't happen."

"To us once buried means always buried," Johnno shouted.

"So you will kill us just to protect your little secret," Julie asked.

"Men have been killed before," Johnno told her.

"Farthingay," Alex cried. "Jeremiah Farthingay was found stabbed to death in that river in the 1800s, was he killed by the Brotherhood?"

"The very first one," Paul told him. "He had realised where the cavern was and our records show that he died to protect the cause, which of course I'm afraid so will you."

"But we won't tell anyone," Julie cried. "No one needs to know."

"You know Girl," Paul replied. "I almost believe you, but it's out of our hands, now if you would be so good to show us how you got out of there, we can't be having it left wide open to the public now can we."

Peter bent down and grabbed hold of Julie and held a knife to her neck "Any trouble from you and she'll die here and now," he told Alex.

Alex told them that there'll be no trouble and he'd lead them to the opening. They followed him along the path and he showed them the entrance.

"So that's the original passageway," Paul asked him. "Now do you mind going back in there?"

"You're gonna bury us again aren't you?" Julie cried as Peter pushed her down to the hole.

"Believe me I am sorry about this," Paul told her. "But it's out of our hands."

"How did you find us?" Alex asked as he bent down to enter the hole.

"It wasn't hard," Paul replied. "For the last 150 years, one of our Orders has been checking out the mountain and the tunnels every night looking for glory seekers like you."

"We're not glory seekers, we are historians, and we have no interest in the gold or jewels."

"Everybody's interested in gold and jewels," Johnno shouted back.

"Not us," Julie pleaded. "We have money, more money than we could ever spend."

"Then why come here?"

"Because it's family," Alex shouted. "She followed me on my grandfather's quest to find the Rainhill Trials so we needed to finish her ancestor's quest, to see if it was real, we don't need money or gold we just needed to see it."

"You can't kill us for something you've never seen," Julie pleaded.

"That's the price for disturbing the dead," Owain told her. "Now get in that tunnel."

"Surely you must be curious," Paul asked. "Your families have been guarding this mountain for generations and you tell me that you have no interest in seeing what you were supposed to be guarding."

The four men looked at one another, all with the same thought running through their heads. "Think about it," Alex told them. "You could be the first of your families ever to see the treasures that you have so dearly guarded and killed for.

"I suppose it can't do any harm," Owain said.

"Yeah," cried Johnno. "I'm up for it."

"It'll make sense," Peter told them. "We can nip inside have a look and kill them in there and then cave the tunnel in, no one would know."

"I suppose it'll be okay," Paul said. "After all, it's not like we have anyone to report to."

So they all agreed and with Alex and Julie leading they re-entered the passageway and made their way back to the cavern. Where the first thing they saw was Gabriel's body still clinging onto the Golden Bell of Mordred.

"That poor soul there," Alex told them. "Was Gabriel Farthingay, the last in the line of Jeremiah Farthingay's family, he died here just like his ancestor."

"He shouldn't have come here then should he," Paul shouted back as he bent down to look at the bell.

"Whatever you do," Alex told them. "Do not touch that bell."

Johnno looked at him "I'm serious mate," Alex told him. "Don't go there."

"We need more light," Paul cried. "These torches aren't much used."

"Well, we did have a generator running those lamps but some idiot cut us off," Julie told him.

"We can fix that," Peter replied. "If we really do want a proper look then why don't we re-connect it, surely between us we can move that stone a bit for girly here to slip through."

"It's an idea," Paul replied. "And seeing as we are here we might as well have a proper look. You lead us to the tomb."

"It's this way," Alex told him as he set off up the passageway. "Tell me something. Why did you kill my car? Do you know how many cars I've lost on this journey?"

"You won't have any more need for it anyway," Paul replied. "Now shut up and show us the passageway."

"Watch the wooden supports," Alex shouted as he heard one of the men behind him walk into one. "If one of them goes then it'll all collapse."

"Watch where you go," Paul told the others. "We don't wanna cave it in just yet."

"Up those steps," Alex told him as he shone his torch up to show the blocked up crypt. "But we'd never move it, it's way too heavy."

"Never say never," Paul replied. "We have a lot of weight between us and we've only got to move it about two feet then your lady would be able to squeeze through and reconnect the generator."

Alex and Julie stood back and watched while the four men struggled with moving the slab. They were astounded to hear it creaking as they managed to lift it up and slide it over a few feet.

"Told you we'd do it," Paul shouted down to Alex. "It just goes to prove that the Welsh are stronger than you puny English."

"Four against one doesn't compare," Julie replied in a huff. "Besides you lot are a tad fatter than my Alex."

Alex tried to hush her as he feared that they'd hit her to shut her up, but he needn't have worried they just laughed at her and admired her guts in the way that she still answered them back even though she knew that they were going to kill her anyway.

"Right, Princess Leia," Paul laughed. "If you don't mind, do you think you can get your tight butt through there?"

Julie looked towards Alex who nodded and told her he'd be alright. As she walked up the steps and tried to squeeze through, Johnno grabbed her backside and pretended to push her up and smiled towards Alex. "She's sure got a hot arse," he laughed as he could see Alex getting annoyed.

The next second, he got a kick in the face from Julie's left foot and he went crashing down the steps "Keep your bloody hands to yourself," Julie shouted as she came back down. "Do you think I'm one of the local sheep?"

Johnno got up holding his back "You broke me back, you stupid bitch," he shouted. "I was only having a bit of fun."

"Calm down Johnno," Paul told him. "It's only a bloody scratch, now can we carry on we haven't got all night."

Alex smiled at Johnno who was still holding his back and moaning while Julie squeezed through the gap into the Tomb. Within a couple of minutes, they heard the generator start up, and then they saw light coming from the cavern's entrance."

"She's done it," Owain shouted as he ran to inspect the cavern. Paul and Alex waited for Julie to re-join them before they too made their way up the passage and into the cavern.

163

"Look at all these riches," Peter shouted as he waded through the treasures scattered over the floor. "These must be worth millions."

"It doesn't matter what they're worth," Paul told him. "It's not ours to sell, Beware the Greedy Man, that's our motto. Our ancestors were chosen because they were honest, trustworthy, good people; we knew what we were signing on for when we all swore the oath to our fathers, who had sworn the oath to their fathers and so on. We are here to protect it, to make sure that the greedy man doesn't find it."

"I wasn't saying that we sell it," Peter replied. "I was just saying that it must be worth a lot."

"Alex," Julie cried as she spotted something on the far wall. "Come quick."

"What is it?" he asked as he joined her.

"It's a painting of some kind," she told him. "It's very faint but you can still make it out."

"It must be what the knights did before they died," Alex cried as he started to rub the green mould of the wall to reveal more and more of the painting. "Julie, give me a hand, it seems to be covering the full wall."

"How come you didn't see that the last time you were down here?" Peter asked them.

"We might have done," Julie replied sarcastically. "But some moron turned the lights off didn't they."

Peter smiled at her and turned his attention to the goodies on the floor as Alex and Julie returned to the wall. As they carefully scraped the moss from the wall, their captors inspected the cavern and all its wonders. Paul knelt down by Gabriel's body to check his pulse.

Then on confirming that he was indeed dead he moved over to what he presumed was the remains of King Arthur. He picked up the shield and looked at the engraving on it and then picked up the sword which had the same engraving.

"So this be Excalibur then?" he shouted to Alex.

"We think it is," Alex replied. "It has the same insignia as the shield and the armour that is by its side, that I believe is all that remained of King Arthur. His body was now just dust."

"I'm sorry about your friend," Paul told him as he got to his feet and walked over to the wall that Alex and Julie were working on. He looked at their faces as they revealed more and more of the brightly coloured painting on the wall. "Do you think that's important?" he asked them. "After all, you're not going to live to show it to anyone."

Julie stopped scraping and stared towards him "Why must we die?" she asked. "We're not interested in taking anything out of here, we're just here to prove to ourselves that it did truly exist, but if we must die then I want to see this painting all of it."

"What do you think it was?" Owain asked as he walked over to them and gazed at the ever-widening painting.

"I don't know for sure, the writings in Latin and it's not a language I specialise in. It looks like it depicts a battle," Alex told him. "Maybe Arthur's final battle."

"Against his son Mordred," Owain replied.

Alex looked at him, surprised that he knew of Arthur's son. "You know about Mordred?" he asked him back.

"Course we do," Peter told him. "Do you think that we'd spend all our lives guarding something and not even bother learning the legend, that's the first thing our fathers told us?"

"That's Mordred there," Paul cried as he pointed to a gold-mask-wearing figure in the painting.

"That mask is down there," Alex told him as he stared at the figure in the painting.

"Are you sure?" Owain asked him as he bent down to pick up the mask. "Can this truly be the Gold Mask that Mordred wore as a child?"

"It must be," Paul told him as he also looked at the figure in the painting. "But it's too small for the one depicted here."

"The one in the painting must be the adult version," Owain told him. "This one must be the one he wore as a child; the legend stated that he always wore a mask from childhood to adulthood."

"It doesn't matter either way," Paul shouted. "It could be the bleeding mask of Zorro for all I care, all I know is that it's stopping here with the rest of the gold."

"I wasn't going to take it, we all know what must be done," Owain replied as he put the mask back down on the floor and walked over to Gabriel's body which still had the golden bell by his side.

"Don't touch that," Alex shouted. "If you know your history. Do not touch that bell."

"It's got an engraving on it," Owain told him as he knelt beside it."

"Gabriel was cleaning the muck of it when he died," Alex replied. "Can you make out what it says?"

"Yes," Owain told him. "It's some kind of warning. IF THOU HAD DRAWN THE SWORD OR RAISED SHIELD THOU HAD BEEN UNLUCKIEST MAN EVER BORN."

"It's a warning to heed," Paul cried. "Come on we've wasted enough time already, we've seen all there is to see."

"So it's time for us to die?" Alex cried as he looked over to Paul.

"We have to protect the secret of the cavern," Paul told him. "If that means killing then so be it."

"Have you actually ever killed anyone?" Julie asked.

"Not actually," Owain replied. "Why?"

"Look at the size of your knife," she told him. "With that thing, you'd have to stab us about sixty times to kill us."

"Not if we cut your throat," Paul shouted. "Now come on let's do this."

"You're not making things any better," Alex cried as he grabbed Julie's hand.

"Better," she shouted. "It can't exactly get any worse."

"Both of you get down to your knees," Paul cried. "Owain you got a knife, do it, do it now."

Owain pushed Julie to her knees and lifted the blade up to her neck "Sorry about this love," he whispered. "But you should have got away when you had the chance."

"Do me first," Alex shouted. "I couldn't bear to watch her die, do me first."

Paul nodded towards Peter who had the other knife "We'll do you both together."

"I'm not doing it," Peter replied as he threw the knife to the floor. "You do it, leave me out of it."

"You swore an oath," Paul shouted. "Now be a man and kill him."

"I never signed on to kill," Peter shouted back. "We are meant to protect the mountain, not end innocent lives."

"They ceased to be innocent when they opened the tomb."

"If he's not doing it, then neither am I," Owain shouted as he handed the knife to Johnno."

"I'm not doing it, I'm no murderer," Johnno replied as he handed the knife to Paul. "You do it."

"You know what I'm like near blood," Paul told him as he dropped the knife.

"Can't we just leave them here and block them in," Peter cried. "That way none of us will have killed them, it would be left to nature."

"We've tried it," Paul told him. "They got out; we can't risk them telling anyone."

"Surely there must be another way?" Julie pleaded. "You can't just kill us; you don't seem to be killers to me."

"It's not our choice love," Johnno told her. "This cavern has to be kept a secret what else can we do."

"There is a way," Alex told him. "To keep this a secret and for us to live."

"Go on then professor," Paul cried. "Enlighten us and it better be good because both your lives are at stake."

"Looking at you I know that you don't really want to kill us," Alex told them. "But I know that you can't have us going free and telling people, but maybe we can help each other."

"You help us," Johnno cried. "How?, Are you gonna kill yourselves?"

"I keep telling you, no one has to die; we don't want anyone to discover this as well."

"You don't," Paul asked. "You mean you travelled all over Wales for clues to a place that once you found it you were gonna forget about it and block it back up, why?"

"We were never in it for glory and gold," Alex replied. "All we wanted to do was to prove that her ancestor's journal was real, she followed me on my grandfather's quest to prove that the Rainhill Trials picture existed and that's why we are here, not for the treasure but to follow her ancestor's clues, we were in it for the chase, that's what we do, we don't need the money for we've both got more than we could ever spend.

I know that you are men of honour so I won't waste my time on offering you money for our lives. We are like you; we followed our family's path to end up here, in the middle of your family's quest to keep it hidden.

"But our quest is the same, Concerve didn't want it to go to the people of power he left word in his journal that it should only be given to the people of Wales and only when they were ready for it, I know that if we disclosed what we found then the people wouldn't receive any benefit from it, we also realise that the people in power would use it for their own benefit."

167

"And we are people of Trust," Julie told them as she interrupted Alex. "You can count on us to keep this place a secret, the clues that we followed are no longer in place, and there is no chance that anyone else could find this place."

"Well, not by the way we did," Alex told them. "There will always be a slight chance that eventually it'll be discovered but that is why you lot are here, to prevent that from ever happening. I'm not asking you to break your vow, I would never ask that of anyone, but I think I know of a way that we can work together to make it even harder for anyone to find it."

"Well, you got me interested," Paul replied. "What was it, how can we hide it even better than before?"

Alex pulled out his notebook and drew a diagram of the cavern and the entrance they used originally by the way of Brones' Tomb. He told them that if they collapsed the tunnel that leads from the tomb to the first passage then there would be no way for anyone to get to the cavern. And to throw people off the scent of the cavern they could easily make it look like Brones' tomb was a tomb.

All it would take was for them to carry the remains of John Brones and place them at the bottom of the steps below the well. Anyone on finding it would just think it to be a nineteenth-century burial ground and not an Arthurian one. It would be easy to make it look like his crypt all we would have to do was to collapse the tunnel from this side by tying a rope to one of the supports and pulling it down once we were safely in the clear.

Then once we are out we can go back to the tomb from the railway tunnel, break back into it, go down the steps from that way and smooth down the collapsed wall. No one would ever realise what lay beyond Brones' body.

"It could work," Owain cried.

"And you two promise that you'd never say a word," Paul asked them.

"Why should we," Julie told him. "We were gonna split the money between certain charities but now that he's dead all his money is gonna be split between the charities."

"What would we do with him?" Paul asked as he looked down at Gabriel's body.

"Leave him there," Alex replied. "It's what he would have wanted."

"Is it a deal?" Julie asked as she offered Paul her hand.

"We'll have to discuss it," Paul told her as he looked over to the others. "It's not my decision."

Alex looked nervously over to Julie and held her hands as the four men whispered between them. Alex could sense that the men actually seemed relieved that they wouldn't have to kill them. Both he and Julie sighed with relief as they agreed that they would do as Alex had told them.

They didn't have a rope with them but Owain had seen an old car tow chain that had been dumped in the car park near to where Alex car was. While he and Peter went to collect it the others set about making the tomb.

Alex got the gruesome task of moving the remains of John Brones and Julie set up two of the spot lamps in the tomb leaving one behind to see what they were doing. While they were doing that the other two looked for the best support to pull down.

"It'll have to be one right in the middle of the passage," Paul shouted.

"Will one support be enough?" Julie asked. "What if it didn't collapse?"

"Then we'll move on to the next," Johnno told her.

"And then the next and then the next," Paul replied. "Until the bugger does fall."

"Right," Alex shouted as he caught back up to them. "That's poor old Brones in place; now let's hope that the chain is long enough."

Just then they heard a cry from the cavern. The two men had returned dragging behind them a very rusty looking tow chain. It was quite long, about 15 feet in length.

"Here," cried Paul. "See if it's long enough to go round both these centre supports."

Alex grabbed the end of the chain and wrapped it around both the supports and then dragged it back towards the cavern. "Right," he shouted. "It should only take two of us to pull it, so the rest of you best get out while you can, we don't know what effect it's gonna have on the rest of the passageways, even the cavern might collapse so you best get all the way out."

"I'll stay with you," Julie told him.

"No, you don't luvvy," Owain told her. "I'm the strongest here, it's gonna be me and him, you are going out with the rest."

"I'm not leaving you," Julie told Alex. "What if it all caves in and you can't get out."

"I'll be alright," Alex replied as he kissed her. "Remember I'm only scared of heights and this will be nothing compared to what we had already been through, take her out," he told Paul as he turned to face the supports.

"We'll give you five minutes, and then we'll pull," Owain shouted as they scrambled down the passageway.

After they were sure that the others had got clear they both looked at one another and nodded. They then took a deep breath and rubbed their hands together before wrapping the chain around their wrists and slowly moving back until the chain went tight.

"Are you ready?" Owain cried.

Alex nodded and they both started to move back towards the cavern. They dug their heels into the gritty earth floor and pulled with all their might. At first, nothing happened but then suddenly they heard one of the supports start to creak.

"Harder," Owain shouted. "It's going."

The next second, the support gave way, and both men lost their footing and slipped to the floor. For a second, they panicked until they realised that nothing had happened. The support had given way, but the passageway was still solid. They had no option but to try again on another support.

Again the support snapped but no cave-in followed. In all, it took five supports to give way before the first sign of falling earth. They both took another deep breath and rubbed their hands again before trying on the sixth one.

This time a lot more earth fell into the passageway just in front of them and just as they were about to try another support they heard a massive roar and the roof of the passageway began to give way. They both dropped the chain and scrambled for their lives into the cavern. There was no way that they could make it into the passage to the outside, so they both huddle on the floor next to the armours of the old knights as a cloud of dust entered the cavern.

After about five minutes, the rumbling stopped and once the dust had settled Alex cried out to see if Owain was alright. Luckily it had only been dust that had entered the cavern and not rocks or earth. They both got to their feet and dusted themselves down before going over to the passageway to see how much damage they had caused.

It looked perfect; the complete passageway had gone buried under tons of collapsed earth. They turned to face one another and shook each other's hands on a job well done. As Owain entered the tunnel to freedom, Alex told him that he wanted a final look around and to say a last farewell to Gabriel and Arthur before joining him.

Once outside the tunnel, Alex almost got knocked into the river below him by an overenthusiastic Julie who was overcome with emotion at seeing her husband make it to safety. While Alex and Owain took a much-needed breather the others worked on hiding their exit tunnel. They dug at it with their bare hands until it caved in and once they were sure that it was unrecognisable as an entrance they made their way back through the railway tunnel to the memorial room.

They quickly removed the still wet cemented bricks from the wall and entered the tomb of Brones for a final time. After about an hour they had completed their task, and from inside the tomb, no one would ever have guessed that there once was a passageway there.

Within another hour, they had removed the tools, the generator, and the remaining spot lamps and had all gathered outside the tunnel. While Johnno and Peter bricked up the entrance again the rest of them sat down on the grass outside the tunnel looking over the river as the daylight began to creep over the facing mountains.

"Sorry about your car," Paul told them.

Alex smiled and grabbed hold of Julie's hand "Don't worry about it," he replied.

"It's not the first car we lost this year," Julie told him as both she and Alex began to laugh.

"What's so funny?" Paul asked them.

"A private joke," Julie told him as they watched the sunrise before them.

A little while later Johnno and Peter joined them as they had finished bricking up the opening.

"How does it look?" Paul asked them.

"Right as rain," Owain told him.

"I take it you two will need a lift back to the hotel?" Johnno asked Alex and Julie.

"Well, they can't take their car, can they," Paul laughed.

"Thanks for not killing us," Julie told them as she got to her feet.

"Yeah, it's much appreciated," Alex cried as he dusted the dirt from his pants.

"We're just guardians," Paul replied. "We can't be bothered with this killing stuff, but we'll need to talk before you go, just to make sure that no one will be coming looking for that fellow in there."

"It'll be fine," Alex told him as they walked back to the main road where they had left their cars.

As they walked towards the car park, Julie looked back towards the tunnel and cried out to Alex as she saw a big black crow. It was sat on the very spot where they had just been sitting. She pointed it out to Alex and the same thought rushed into both their heads.

Could that be Arthur reincarnated as a crow as predicted centuries ago? They both smiled and looked at one another and shook their heads. As they set off in separate cars, they all agreed to have a shower and a nap before meeting up again in the evening at the Cwellyn Arms to discuss the Gabriel matter.

While Alex was having a shower he shouted to Julie that he had something to tell her but by the time he had dried himself down she was asleep on the bed snoring her little head off. He smiled at her and then joined her on the bed and cuddled into her.

They awoke about four in the afternoon and while Julie had a shower Alex made her a brew.

"I can't believe that after all, we've been through we haven't got anything to remind us of the cavern," Julie told him as she dried her hair while sat on the end of the bed.

"Not exactly," Alex replied. "I did get you this."

"What is it?" she cried out excitedly as Alex pulled something from his pants pocket.

"I saw you looking at it when Gabriel had hold of it," he replied as he pulled out a small golden bracelet which was embraced with silver and crystals.

"My God," she cried as she snatched it from his hand. "When did you get that?"

"After the cave-in," he told her. "Owain left me alone so I grabbed that, and I also took a few snaps on the camera on my phone."

"Let's see," she asked as he gave her his phone to show her close up photos of the dead knights, the cross, the bell, the wall painting and a few surrounding shots. "They are for us only no one else must ever see them."

"There is no one else to show my love; you are all that I have."

"Ditto," he replied.

"What was in the envelope?" she asked him.

"What envelope?" he replied.

"The one Gabriel gave you."

"Bloody hell I forgot about, where's my jacket?"

She handed him his jacket and he pulled out the envelope and opened it to reveal a small handwritten letter and some legal papers.

"They look important," she told him as she picked up the legal papers. "Bloody hell they've got the deeds to his flat in Cardiff, what's that about?"

"Listen to this," Alex told her as he read out the hand-written letter.

My dear friends.

In case I didn't make it out of the cavern I have written this letter to ask you to do me one last favour. Before he died Joseph told me that he killed a young girl in the village where he was born. He buried her body and as far as he knew there was no way that she would ever be discovered. He told me that on the night he killed her he placed her body in an open grave and covered her up with some earth.

The next day the open grave was used and filled. so somewhere In the village of Eldersfield Gloucestershire, there is a distraught Family mourning their missing daughter. I want you both to go to the village and talk with your parents. It shouldn't take you too long to discover their names. The way he spoke about his village I got the impression that it wasn't very big.

If that was the case then it should only have a small graveyard if So then once you have discovered the family they would tell you the date she disappeared and then surely there can't have been many burials the day after.

I blame myself for what happened to Joseph and maybe by you Finding the girl's body, maybe I will find solace in where ever I end up. I have total faith in your abilities, after all, if you can find a burial chapel after 1500 years then finding a girls grave after a couple should be a piece of cake.

I have enclosed the deeds to my Cardiff flat, there are no keys Just key in 1852 into the keypad in the door and you will gain entrance. The flat is totally paid for and as I've no need for it anymore then it's yours, enjoy the view it's situated over the bay, make use of it more than I did.
Yours,
Gabriel Farthingay.

"He must have planned to die in there," Julie cried.

"Well, he was dying," Alex told her. "I guess every man should be allowed to choose their own resting place."

"Well, at least now we can have a proper honeymoon, just you and me and the view over Cardiff Bay."

They spent the evening with the Brotherhood of the Light Beings, and after assuring them that no one else would be searching for it, they bid them goodbye and retired for the night.

The next day they got Johnno to run them over to a friend of his who had a car for sale. A 1987 red Vauxhall Corsa. They then set off for the village of Eldersfield in Gloucestershire to fulfil Gabriel's last wish.

It took them almost seven hours to drive through the middle of Wales and once in the village they quickly discovered the identity of the parents of the missing girl. They soon found their address and pulled up in the lane next to their house. They left the car, and after taking a couple of deep breaths, they walked hand in hand up the path and rang the doorbell.

The End

EXCALIBUR'S GOLD

A couple's search through the historical wonders of the Welsh countryside for clues to the greatest discovery of all time

KING ARTHUR

Join them as their search takes them from the Pontcysyllte Aqueduct near Llangollen to the Devil's Bridge via the shoreline Chapel of St Govan's in Pembrokeshire all because of a clue, they found in an old painting of the Britannia Bridge on Anglesey.